TWO BY TWO
David Garnett

For his new novel, David Garnett has taken a story from the beginning of the world, one of the most charmingly dramatic – and, incidentally, one of the best documented – stories of the Old Testament, that of The Flood. In minutest detail, he has reconstructed a totally credible picture of an event which must, by any standards, have been spectacular.

His two main characters are interpolations, the twins Fan and Niss. These two girls, convinced by Noah's gloomy prophecies regarding the future of mankind, succeed in getting into the Ark as stowaways. In spite of the deluge, the weeks riding the flood, the shortage of food and the problems that arise from living in the animals' quarters, all goes well until they are discovered; and it is only when the Ark grounds on Mount Ararat that they are able to escape into a pristine, if still wet, world. Here, with the help of two of Noah's grandsons, they set out upon their travels.

Although Mr Garnett's story was not conceived as a parable of the dangers we live in today, it could be regarded as one. Certainly it is among the most vividly enchanting of all his novels.

D1643527

Two by Two

A STORY OF SURVIVAL BY

David Garnett

LONGMANS, GREEN AND CO LTD
48 Grosvenor Street, London W.1

Associated companies, branches and representatives
throughout the world

© *David Garnett, 1963*
First published 1963

Printed in Great Britain by
Northumberland Press Limited
Gateshead on Tyne

To

Frances Olivia Garnett

and

Nerissa Stephen Garnett

PREFACE

What follows is a story taken from the beginning of the world. But it is one which many people living today appear to believe may be repeated in another form. I am told they are building arks in the backyards of every state in the Union and that any stowaways will be warmly received.

In this scientific age the story of the Deluge raises many questions. How did the plants fare? What did the herbivorous animals eat until the grass grew again? How did the carnivora manage to wait until their natural prey had obeyed the Divine command to be fruitful and multiply?

We are told that the olive trees kept their foliage after an immersion of nearly five months, but we know that the survivors, if any, of a modern counterpart of the Deluge will find little vegetation upon the earth and that the surviving animals may be sterile like the turtles of Bikini atoll. So on all counts it will be better not to repeat the exploits of Niss and Fan.

But though this book will be taken, inevitably, as a parable for the times we live in, I must ask the reader to believe that it was not written as such. It was conceived as a frivolous gloss upon the most charming story in the Bible. But only after many pages had been written did I find that a parable kept pushing its way in.

D.G.

Part One

I N the days before the Flood, when even the smallest babies were antediluvian, there was a pair of twins who were nobody's business. Their father was old even for those days and claimed that when he was a boy he had stolen apples from a tree grown from a pip that Eve had saved when she was turned out of Eden. Their mother had been a girl friend of Methuselah's before her marriage. Then father and mother died leaving twin orphan girls in a little town which was washed away soon after this story begins. Nobody now knows where it was. But there were great mountains to the north and a fertile plain stretching to the sea. The people who lived in the town were mostly short dark men with black greasy hair and curly beards and the women had big flashing eyes and big hips and bosoms, and were fat and jolly, always generous but never careless. The twins belonged to a different type; they grew up tall and slinky, had grey eyes and brown hair which bleached gold in the sun and their skins burned pale gold or red but never dusky or black. They were always careless and only generous to people they liked.

As there was no one to bother about them, they

learned early to make their own plans and live their own life, though they often quarrelled about what that was to be.

One spring when they were fourteen they got bored with all the people in the town so they decided to follow the flocks of sheep and goats which stayed in the hills until the grazing was exhausted. They walked fast and about midday they overtook a man called Phil who was a great wolf hunter, sitting by the side of the road. He had with him a dog which was a famous tracker: a small yellow-red dog with a bushy tail almost like a fox's. He offered them some bread and raw onions which they accepted and sat down by the road to eat. When they had finished eating all three went on together, the twins in front. They had slings and kept hurling pebbles at any mark such as a tree or a rock, which took their fancy. Phil followed behind with a pack of food on his back and a big boar spear in his hand, a sharp hunting knife in his girdle. He had brown eyes, dark hair and a curly black beard. He never whistled or sang, but nodded his head and always said what he meant using as few words as he could.

On the first night he made a fire in a hollow under a high rock which sheltered them from the wind and hid the flames from any prying eyes.

Phil brought out dry unleavened bread, dry milk, some dates and a skin of very strong wine which the inventor, old Noah, had given him in exchange for the promise of a pair of wolf cubs. He shared the food equally with Niss and Fan, but they were suspicious of the wine and refused it and drank from a pool under the rock.

Next morning they went up the mountain and by midday came to a slope dotted with white sheep: ewes and their lambs. The old shepherd who had watched them approaching came a few yards down the hill to meet them.

'You are welcome,' he said. 'And your dog is more welcome still. Last night wolves came; our three dogs rushed out and the two best were killed and we are left with one coward dog hopping on three legs. I am alone here with one young boy for I sent my eldest son into the valley to fetch help.'

'How many wolves were there?' asked Phil.

'I think that there were three,' answered the old shepherd. 'And two of them would be she-wolves with cubs.'

'I am a hunter by trade. What will you pay me to kill these wolves?' asked Phil.

'The sheep are not mine. But my master would pay you a lamb for every wolf.'

Phil laughed and picked up his pack as though to go on his way.

'Three unbranded lambs weaned from the ewe, for every wolf,' he said.

'Two,' said the old shepherd.

'Three,' repeated Phil.

'Well, three for every grown wolf and one lamb for every cub.'

[5]

Phil agreed to this. They sat down and drank ewe's milk.

After a time Phil and the old shepherd started up the mountain and Niss and Fan followed them. The little boy and the dog hopping on three legs were driving the sheep down from the higher slopes and there was a great noise of baaing. Presently the old shepherd stopped at a place where there were tufts of wool scattered about and Fan and Niss could see where a ewe had stood at bay and a few yards further was her mangled body. A torn-off little woolly leg was all that remained of her lamb. David, the red dog, whined. The hair was bristling all up his back. Phil put him on a leather leash which he gave to Niss to hold, and the dog set off across the hillside dragging her after him, towards a cliff. Once or twice Phil pointed to wisps of wool which had been caught on pointed stones.

'Torn off the lamb she was carrying,' he said.

Fan was angry. She thought that she ought to be holding David and that she would do it better than her sister. She took a polished pebble out of her mouth and set it in her sling.

David led them to a cleft in the cliff face. There was a ledge running up to a hole in the cliff, level with Phil's head. He climbed up balancing himself with his spear. The old man held his legs while he looked down the hole.

'The she-wolf is up there with her cubs,' said

Phil. 'The best thing we can do is to smoke them out.'

They all began to gather dry grass and heather. Soon a fire was blazing in the cleft below the ledge where the wolf had her den. Phil smothered it with peat. The wind blew the smoke into the cleft. After half an hour David began whining and straining at his leash.

'Look out! Here she comes,' said Phil.

There was a sudden rush above them, and one after another two wolves leapt from the ledge. Phil caught the first wolf on his spear; the second animal knocked down the old shepherd who was close under the cliff tending the fire. It slashed his thigh in a wicked bite; bolted round a rock and disappeared. Niss was clinging to David's leash holding him back from attacking the great she-wolf which Phil was pinning back against the cliff with his spear. The blade had gone through its chest and had come out between the shoulder blade and the spine. The wolf bit at the shaft of the spear and splinters flew out. Phil called to her: 'Quick, hold on here.' She let go of David's leash and the dog vanished. She grabbed the handle of the spear and threw all her weight into keeping the wounded animal pinned to the rock. As she leant forward the wolf's jaws were not more than a yard from her; its eyes were fixed on hers with desperate intensity, its mouth was full of blood and splinters and then the great teeth bit again into the shaft below the head of the spear, which twisted to one side. It was almost severed from the haft, it broke and she fell forward on to the wolf. But just as she pitched forward, Phil drove his hunting knife through the ribs into the wolf's heart and as Niss fell on it the only living things left were the eyes still fixed on her. Afterwards she thought that in those eyes she had recognised herself. She and the dying wolf were one. Each of them at that moment was all important to the other. She felt no pity for the wolf and no regret; but she knew that henceforward she could be a wolf if need be. The knowledge frightened her.

Fan had been standing behind when the wolves came out, ready to take part when called upon. After the wolves sprang she and David were the only ones to notice that two wolf cubs, not more than eighteen inches long, had tumbled off the ledge and run away round the rock after the wolf that had slashed the old shepherd. Fan rushed after them, fixed her eye on one of the creatures, whirled her sling and the pebble hit it fair and square, breaking its back. Fan rushed after it as it dragged itself, paddling with its front paws and dragging the paralysed hind ones. She had no weapon but picked up a rock and hit at it. Her blow missed and the little creature struggled on, a second time she missed and then hit its skull, holding the rock in her hands, and battered the cub until it lay still with drops of blood runing from the tip of its nose.

David had killed the other cub. ' I wanted those cubs

for old Noah,' said Phil. 'But we may find some others.' He tore up the old shepherd's shirt to bind up his thigh. Then when he had done his best to staunch the blood, he carried the old man on his back with Fan walking behind holding his legs. By the time they had got him down the hillside, they met his son leading a party headed by the owner of the herd.

The events of the evening had to be explained and it was dark before Phil said: 'Well, I've earned five unbranded lambs, weaned from the ewes. I'll pick them out and put my own brand on them tomorrow.'

The farmer glared angrily. 'You are a greedy fellow. You ought to be grateful for our showing you sport. I'll pay no lambs.'

'You pay me those lambs or . . .' said Phil.

'So you threaten me. You damned outlaw. Get you gone.' And the farmer and the men with him stood up grasping their spears.

'If you hadn't come along we should have killed those wolves ourselves and Eli would not have received his deathwound. And you have the audacity to claim five lambs.'

Phil's spearhead was in his pouch. The splintered useless shaft stood against a rock.

'Enough said,' and Phil smiled, showing his teeth as he uttered the words. 'Come on Fan. Wake up Niss. We aren't wanted here.'

Fan picked up the body of the wolf cub she had killed.

'Put that down, girl,' said the shepherd's son, aiming his spear at her. 'That's our wolf.'

'I killed it,' said Fan, glaring at him coldly.

'You be off, or I'll be having your life for my father's,' said the youth prodding her with his spear point. Fan dropped the dead cub, stepped back and joined the others. They set off in the dark, climbing, stumbling over loose stones and at last got into a scrub forest of dwarf rhododendrons above the high pasture. Phil lit a fire and when each of them had taken a nip of Noah's wine, he burned out the bit of wood in the socket of his bronze spear-head and then pressed the shaft into the hot socket and began to bind it in with some strips of raw hide.

While he worked, for the first time he talked freely.

'Bad dishonest people. They ought to be swept off the face of the earth. I had to watch that boy prod you – a girl – with his spear. One day I'll be even with him.'

'Hope the dog wolf comes back for more lambs,' said Fan.

'No, that is wrong,' said Phil gravely. 'We are men and must side together against the animals.'

Later, when they had eaten, Fan went back to the argument.

'I don't see why we should side with man under all circumstances just because we happen to be human.'

'Suppose there is an animal nobler than man,' said Niss.

'There are many. Horses for example,' said Phil.

'Well, in that case I side with the horse and not with its rider. And the wilder and more vicious it is, the more I admire it,' said Fan. Niss nodded agreement.

'Man has to stand by man,' said Phil.

'But suppose . . .' Niss did not finish what she was going to say which was: 'Suppose I were to become a wolf?' for she realised that Phil was a wolf hunter and that wolves were his special enemies. They slept round the wood fire, Phil and David on one side, Fan and Niss on the other. Suddenly they were woken up by Phil's calling out 'David! David!' It was pitch black; still hours before dawn and the fire had burned down to ash and ember.

'Where is David gone?'

They sat up side by side peering into the darkness while Phil rose calling David, then blowing the embers into flame and putting wood on it and calling again. But even when he had a flame he could see nothing to explain why David, who had been sleeping against his ankles, should have disappeared. Soon he lay down again and the sun had risen before the two girls woke up again to find that Phil was also absent.

They built up the fire and made themselves a meagre breakfast of dried milk stirred into hot water, and biscuit. They were wandering about not knowing what to do next when Phil came back, his face set with anger.

'Leopard,' he said and stuck his spear in the ground.

[11]

'What do you mean?' asked Niss.

'A snow leopard took David and killed him before he could bark or whine.' Fan and Niss gazed at him with horror.

'A snow leopard. There was blood on the rock where he had eaten him and his track in the mud where he had drunk from the spring afterwards. The blood made him thirsty. I shall stay here now until I have killed him.'

'Can we help?' asked Fan, and Niss nodded her head.

'I shall make a deadfall, but I shall want bait. A live dog is the best. Leopard love eating dog. But I shall make do with a lamb. Those men owe me five lambs. You two girls must bring one of them up here without anybody seeing you, while I make the trap.'

Fan lay on a rock overlooking the pasture slopes watching the shepherd boys bringing up the sheep. Then she saw far below a party of four men, two dragging the old shepherd on a rough litter made of what looked like two hurdles down the mountainside while the other two walked behind with their spears on their shoulders. That meant that one man was being left behind at the camp with the shepherd's son and the young boy. Best of all there was no dog; the lame dog was staying in camp too. Fan smiled as she reflected that they must be confident that they had frightened Phil away. Also they had seen his spear shaft, but they did not know that he had the head in his pouch and that his first action had been to set the head on. An hour after the party had gone down the mountain, she saw a man come out from the bivouac and wave and soon afterwards the shepherd's son and the boy went down the hillside. This was the opportunity they had been waiting for and she waved to Niss, further up the hill, who came down slowly, picking her way among the rocks. She went past Fan and into a hollow and disappeared. Ten minutes later she came into sight again carrying a white object in her arms and began climbing the hill. She had not got far when a sheep dashed after her and then ran, first on one side of her and then on the other.

No one had seen Niss coming back and Fan slipped off the rock to find that Phil had come down into the hollow and was tying the lamb's legs together with twine. The sheep was looking at them from close to and was excited.

Phil took his spear, aimed carefully and threw it at the ewe. The bronze blade of the spear caught her in the side and went in and the weight of the spear knocked her over. Before she could stagger to her legs Phil had caught her and driven his hunting knife into her throat. The blood gushed out over his hands.

'Why did you kill her?' asked Niss.

'She would have hung about all night and have sprung my leopard trap. Besides, we want meat.'

Niss nodded gravely. They were good reasons. But she would have liked to have kept the ewe. After all the leopard might not come and how could they feed the lamb if it did not?

They were eating roast cutlets and throwing the bones into the fire when Phil asked them:

'Do you know the penalty for sheep stealing?'

Fan and Niss looked at him blankly.

'Impaling. The executioner drives a stake through your navel.'

'How did you make your deadfall for the leopard?' asked Fan changing the subject. For Phil had forbidden them to go anywhere near his trap. 'The less scent of man the better,' he had declared.

Now he turned to give an explanation.

'I tie up the lamb in the middle of a thorn bush so that it looks as though it might have been caught in it naturally. Just out of reach of the lamb, but where the leopard must pass to reach it is the trigger sticking out from a flat stone about four inches high. On the trigger is a strong forked stick which supports a flat rock. The leopard cannot get to the lamb without touching the trigger which knocks it off the stone, and down comes stick and rock. The rock may fall too slowly. But I hope it will crush the leopard before he can jump aside.'

Next morning the twins were woken up at dawn by Phil who was standing triumphantly carrying the dead leopard over his shoulder.

'Now we shall see whether I have had my revenge,' he said and kneeling down he slashed at the leopard's belly and dragged the lovely fur apart to show pink muscle. Then he cut down to the stomach and cut that. The first thing they saw were some dark red tufts of wet dog's fur. The leopard had eaten David. Fan gazed spellbound at the sight, but Niss felt queer and turned away. Soon afterwards she was sick. Phil cut out the leopard's stomach and buried it and lifted a flat rock on top.

'That is David's grave. I have buried him decently.' Then he walked back to the leopard grinning in a way which frightened them.

'Look, she is in milk,' he said. And he showed them a thick creamy pink and white layer clotted under the slashed skin. The sight of this disgusted Niss so much that she turned pale and thought she would vomit again.

'We must find the cubs,' said Phil.

'David would have found them in two minutes,' said Fan, and Phil turned on her savagely with parted lips and bare teeth and caught indrawn breath.

Fan stood her ground and a moment later Phil recovered himself and led the way to the deadfall. The rock had fallen directly on the leopard when she had seized the lamb. Phil had to use all his strength to roll it to one side when he pulled out the leopard, but the lamb was still underneath. Now he pulled out the little body: it would still serve as bait. From the trap they walked along the base of the cliff which had broken away into a scree of loose stones. At last they came to an opening in the wall where one could climb the cliff. They climbed precariously. When they were almost at the top they saw a narrow ledge running down sideways. There was a hole below in the rock. Phil put the back of his hand to his mouth and made a strange call. A faint mewing answered him. Then he threw the body of the lamb outside the hole at the end of the ledge and stood with spear poised. They waited motionless for an hour. Fan saw an eagle that soared in great circles along the top of the cliff, balancing in the air and shifting its weight but never flapping a wing. The great primary feathers of the wings stuck out like separate fingers. Niss, whose eyes were on the ground watched a bumble bee which had fallen among the gravel and was torpidly crawling up and then falling back waving its legs.

Suddenly each of them became aware that the cubs were in the entrance of their den. Shifting their eyes and holding their breath, they saw the leopard kits come out, gazing round-eyed and suspiciously at the world. Then with wonderful grace one of the two flung itself on the dead lamb and stood over it growling at the other who followed more uncertainly.

While they watched, Phil struck the trembling, uncertain kitten dead with his spear. At that Niss jumped forward and caught up the growler, though she was poised on the narrow ledge with a drop on to rocks below. In an instant her wrist had been torn with four bloody grooves and she had dropped the little creature which slid over and fell where she nearly followed. By the time she had tip-toed back to safety Phil had run down and was hammering the kitten to death with a rock.

'Why . . . why? You devil.' Niss glowered at him in fury as the pain came and the blood ran down on to her torn smock.

Phil did not answer in words but he recovered his spear, picked up the kittens and led the way back to the fire. Fan and Niss followed in silence. For the first time they were afraid of him. And watching him they felt their uneasy fear growing. Phil picked up the dead leopard and held her up by the neck. She was a creature of beauty and horror, for her bowels dangled from her lovely fur between her hind legs. Phil thrust his face into hers and gloated:

'Your cubs are dead, mashed into a bloody mess. You have been ripped open and David given burial while you will lie on the rocks for the ravens and the crows. You were a fool: a vain and silly fool to pit yourself against Phil the hunter. I have destroyed you as easily as you would destroy a rat.'

That evening Niss and Fan sat further away from Phil and they were silent until Niss said:

'A noble animal, a horse for example, would not gloat over the dead.'

Phil sat silent and did not appear to hear. At last Fan said:

'I would like the skin of the snow leopard.'

'Take it then,' said Phil and held out his knife.

Together Fan and Niss skinned the creature and then rubbed ashes from the fire into the skin to cure it. Fan took the knife back to Phil but he was asleep so she laid it down by his side.

Next morning Phil woke them at the first light before dawn.

'The shepherds will be searching for the lost ewe and her lamb. We must be going. And here our ways part. I go higher into the mountain and you back to where there are streets and people. If you go over the crest and down the other spur of the mountain you will come to the forest and that will lead you down to the village where old Noah lives. He's a fine old chap, gone a bit queer, but he makes wine and he's interested in animals. There's a little town beyond and I guess you'll be safe there.'

Niss and Fan were not sorry to be parting from Phil: ever since David's death the looks he cast on them made them uneasily aware that they were young girls, weaker than a lonely savage man and at the mercy of his moods. What they had seen in his company had shocked them and they needed time in which to recover before they knew what they thought. And Niss's wrist had swollen up and needed soaking in hot water and wrapping in clean rags. So they took his advice and keeping well out of sight of the shepherd's camp, they crossed the crest and went down on the other side of a mountain spur. For a whole day

[18]

they picked their way among rounded ice-worn boulders, between which there were few tufts of thin grass. There were no sheep, no shepherds, nothing to be seen but the wheatear that got up in front of them and flew from stone to stone and was always there twenty yards in front of them so that it seemed as though there was but the one bird on the mountainside that they had been following all day. Once too they heard a deep, hoarse voice and could see high up and very far away, the black speck that was a raven whom they had heard calling to his mate in another valley of the mountains. Next day they saw the line of the forest below them and scrambled down among the stones until they got to the first twisted stunted firs and soon after that the forest swallowed them up and they followed the way that seemed easiest, downhill.

Early in the afternoon they heard the sound of axes and, going towards it, they came into a clearing in the forest with tall foxgloves growing among the tree-stumps. From there they could see framed in the tall cypresses on either side, a mountain village far below them, and they guessed that they were not far off their road. Presently the old clearing with foxgloves and willowherb gave way to where the woodsman's work was recent and they heard the axes again and saw three big men working, one of them squaring a baulk of timber, the others loading a sleigh with huge timbers already shaped and notched. A team of mules was waiting tethered near by.

Niss cried out: 'What cheer!' in her thin voice, but the men, intent on their work did not look up. Leading out of the clearing was a road marked with the runners of the sleigh blue upon the stones. From there they could see the village clearly. Opposite there was a waterfall dropping in a white line from the cliff to the narrow valley below. And clustered together were the village houses, all of wood, with overhanging eaves and orchards stretching down the river banks. Overtopping everything was the unfinished roof of an immense wooden building; a temple perhaps, that could have held all the other houses in the village within its walls. Although it had been built in a flat meadow low down by the stream, it was so big that they could still see the roof when they had got among the houses. The people they saw as they came in to the village were indolent; the women sluttish with their dark hair unbrushed and their placket holes gaping. There were sunflowers in every garden and all the people, men and women as well as children, were perpetually cracking the seeds and spitting out the shucks.

There were women gossiping as Fan and Niss came down the street but nobody bothered to notice them or to give them a greeting and the only person they could see at work was a woman milking a goat.

Then as they went down the steep winding street to the little market place at the bottom of the village they heard the tapping of a hammer and saw a saddler sitting outside his shop driving copper nails into the breeching pad for a shaft horse or mule. Pegged out on the fence of his yard were the hides of a dozen sheep and goats.

The sisters stopped and watched him while he took round-headed copper nails out of his mouth and drove them one by one in a pretty pattern through the leather covering into the wooden frame beneath. When he had driven in the last one he looked at them enquiringly and asked:

'What can I do for you, young women?'

'I was wondering . . .' said Fan.

'I was just watching,' said Niss.

'Do you cure those skins yourself?' asked Fan.

'Yes. I'm a tanner as well as a saddler and a cobbler,' he replied. 'I do all kinds of leather work.'

'How can I cure this skin?' asked Fan and opening her bundle she showed him the skin of the snow leopard.

'What a beauty! Where did you get that?' asked the saddler giving each of them a sharp glance.

'We were up in the mountains with a hunter called Phil,' said Niss. The saddler nodded.

'I know him. Many's the wolfskin I've bought from him. How's his dog David?'

'David's dead. This leopard killed him and ate him,' said Fan.

'I'm sorry to hear that. Well, Phil had his revenge

it seems. I'll get busy on this. It will take a week to get it really supple.'

'Can you find us a job while we are waiting?' asked Fan.

'I can that. I've two hundred and fifty rawhide halters to cut out and stitch for old Noah.'

'Who's Noah? Didn't Phil say something about him?' asked Niss.

'It is he who has built the great ship in the bottom meadows.'

'Ship?' exclaimed Fan and Niss simultaneously.

'Aye. It's made for the water so it be a ship. Looks more like a temple from here.'

'Did Noah build that?' asked Niss.

'He and his three sons have been building it for the last twenty years. They've cut down half the cypresses and cedars on this side of the stream to build it.'

'We came past some men with a sleigh and a mule team as we came out of the forest,' said Fan.

'Aye, that will be his sons: Japheth, Shem and Ham.'

'What's it for?' asked Niss.

'You may well ask. Noah was a rich man once. Then he got the notion that the world was coming to an end and he's been building that thing which he calls an ark, ever since.'

'For twenty years?' said Fan marvelling.

'Just so. But it's hard on his sons. They are getting on now. Japheth must be forty but he's been working as an unpaid carpenter all his life. All three are married and they do a bit of farm work now and again: but all their time and thought go into building that great thing.'

While they were talking there was the jingling of bells and the creaking of strained wood and the mule team came swinging down the village street with the tall fair man with blue eyes leading the mules with their traces slack and two slighter darker men behind pulling on the brakes of the sleigh loaded with four great baulks of timber, each already notched and shaped at the ends.

The saddler greeted them but only Japheth replied. When they were gone a little way the saddler said:

'There you are. Shem is a crafty suspicious fellow and Ham is surly. It's Noah's fault that they have grown up like that.'

'What will you pay us for making bridles?' asked Fan.

'What will you pay me for suppling your leopard skin?'

Fan looked blank for a moment and their new friend laughed.

'I'll give you your food and lodging and pay you piece work. And then I'll take a bit off for the leopard skin.'

'Come along, let's have a look at the ark,' said Fan.

When they had got clear of the village and down to the flat meadows by the stream, they saw what their new acquaintance had meant in calling the great building a ship. It was flat bottomed but it had a rounded prow like an immense barge and the wooden walls went straight up for twenty feet without a break. Above that level there were recessed decks and the huge overhanging incompleted roof. The ark lay in the midst of gardens and orchards: in one place the loaded branches of an apple tree brushed against its side. The tree had grown there since that bit of the ark had been built. And the great wooden wall was so enormous that they couldn't see all of it at once. It just went curving out of sight among the laden fruit trees.

As they walked along marvelling, a woman who was bunching onions, straightened up and shouted at them:

'You clear off. You thieving baggages.'

She was ugly, with a red face and clumsy wooden shoes wearing a dirty blouse and skirt drawn tight over her belly. As Fan and Niss took no notice of her, she began to run towards them so Niss turned to face her.

'I'm not doing any harm,' she said.

'Get out. You've come to steal the Lord's onions, but you'll drown for it.'

Fan and Niss stared, but when the woman made a grab, Niss jumped aside and they ran off laughing.

A man in the roof of the ark stopped hammering to shout as they walked back through the orchard to the saddler's shop, but they were not sure whether he was shouting at them or at two boys they had seen. The two boys followed them and threw stones, but when Fan put a pebble in her sling and sent it whizzing back they ran away.

Noah's family seemed a funny lot of people, they said, after the saddler had shown Fan how to cut out the rawhide nose bands and side cheeks and Niss how to pierce the leather with an awl, so that he himself could stitch the halters together with waxed thread.

'The townspeople come up here now and again, to make trouble. They did talk of burning the ark, and that set Noah's family against everyone. The town people would have burned it once, only it came on to rain in torrents. Noah's family are a bit too ready to boast that God does just what they tell Him and of course they all said that God sent the rain that evening. But Noah himself is a fine old chap, only he drinks too much and his wife is a really fine woman. Japheth is the best of the others.'

During the week that Fan and Niss worked for the saddler, they watched the building of the ark with great interest. Every other day the three brothers took the mule team up into the forest and came back with a load of cypress boards. The roof was being finished and they watched how they were hoisted into position with pulleys and fastened down with oak pegs. 'She's all finished, bar the fitting-out inside,' said Japheth when he came up to take a score of the halters.

On the evening of the Sabbath a crowd of townspeople came up and began to walk round the ark, whistling and shouting, and suddenly old Noah came out and leaning over the bulwarks as from the edge of a pulpit, began to shout at them. And what he had to say was intolerable.

'All of you are abhorred of God. Your lives are wicked: your vices are unmentionable. God will sweep you all away, but He loves me and my children for we are His servants. The rain will come; the waters will rise. Foot by foot it will come into your houses and you will have no refuge. But all the beasts of the field, even the lizards, shall be saved because they are without sin and God has commanded me to take them into this Ark. And while all of ye men and women and the little babies at the breast shall be swallowed up by the waters, the wild cat and her kittens and the wolf and her cubs and the very scorpions on the rocks shall live, for ye are an evil generation and they are good in the eyes of the Lord, set beside you.'

After that the assembled people began to throw rotten tomatoes and then stones, and Shem and Japheth dragged their father down out of sight of the multitude. Then, seeing that there was no more sport to be had, the angry people drifted away.

The bridles were finished and the leopard skin was cured, so Fan and Niss said good-bye to the saddler and walked down to the town which stood where the mountain valley opened into a plain. This was a different world, with its priests and its temple, its markets with fruit and fowls and pigeons and sheep and goats, and its open square with a pillory in the centre with the stocks facing it and the town bailiff walking round with two burly constables with whips at his elbow.

But Fan and Niss soon made a friend in this busy place; he was a black-coated dog with yellow eyebrows and yellow patches behind his ears. He belonged to the owner of a puppet theatre and so through their friendship with the dog Fan and Niss got to talking with the puppet master and were given jobs: Fan to carve the heads of some new puppets out of wood, and to repaint the faces of the old ones when they had got the worse for wear, and Niss to make new dresses for them. One day when the puppet master was giving a show and Fan was making the collection among the audience, a fight started between some boys at the back. She pushed through the crowd quickly and heard boys among the spectators shouting: 'Give it to the Noahs!' A boy wrenched himself free from half a dozen who were holding him and ran off. There was another boy lying on the ground who was being kicked.

Fan hit one of the aggressors in the face. 'Seize him,' she called to the dog. The boy turned to hit her but the dog seized him by the calf of the leg. The boy screamed and next moment his companions had run off. Fan helped up the boy who was lying on the ground and called the dog off the one whom she had hit. His leg was streaming with blood but he hobbled off spitting and swearing revenge. His victim had a

cut lip and was winded and bruised but directly he
had got his breath he gave Fan a wide-open smile
while the blood ran down into the crease of his chin.
Fan liked him.

'I won't throw any more stones at you again,' he
said to her surprise.

'Oh, are you one of the Noah boys?'

'Yes, I'm Mizraim, Ham's son. Gomer and I came
in because of the puppets. But it is none too safe for
us in this town. And my Dad would give me a hiding
if he knew I had come here.'

Niss, who had been selling cups of lemonade came
up then and gave him a drink.

'Well, it's been worth it, meeting you two,' he said
gallantly, handing back the cup from which he had
drunk, smeared with his blood.

'You make the collection, Niss. I'll go with the dog
and see Mizraim on the road in case any of the boys
are lying in wait for him.' Niss nodded, she understood.

After that they went out several times to see the
Ark and the Noahs. At first Ham used to shout out:

'Get out of here, you evil spawn,' but at last they
were tolerated and Mrs Noah even gave them a taste
of her husband's rough red wine. Fan pulled a face at
the acid taste, but Niss drank hers sip by sip and afterwards drank up what was left of Fan's. Soon afterwards she lay down on a heap of shavings in the hot
sun and went to sleep.

The two boys, Gomer and Mizraim, kept out of the sisters' way, for they were forbidden to speak to strangers and Ham often struck his son, though Japheth did not actually beat Gomer. Shem was always nagging and scolding. The wives: Mrs Japheth, Mrs Shem and Mrs Ham, were horrid women and always shouted if they saw Fan or Niss. Only Mrs. Noah was kind in her wooden way.

Summer and autumn and winter went by. Then nine months after they had gone to work for the puppet-master, just after the spring sale of sheep and lambs, a small child ran up and asked: 'Are you Niss and Fan?'

'No, we are Fan and Niss,' answered Fan to whom the child had spoken.

'I have a message for you. A very private, secret message.' The infant paused after these words which he had got by heart.

'Well, what is it?' asked Fan.

'Leave the town tonight. Impalement certain to-morrow.'

'Who gave you this message?'

The infant shook his head. Niss handed him a piece of toffee which she had been given by Mrs Noah. 'Was it the wolf hunter?' she asked. The little boy began to cry and ran away.

Fan and Niss repeated the message to each other. ' "Leave the town tonight. Impalement certain to-morrow!" That can only be from Phil.'

They went back to the village to see their friend the cobbler.

'What's new?' asked Niss.

'They've took Phil, that hunter friend of yours – the one who had that good dog. He's to be impaled for sheep stealing.'

Fan and Niss wandered out without looking at each other.

'Old Ephraim the carrier is leaving the town tonight. Let's go with him,' said Fan. Niss nodded.

They went back to the town to the market place, keeping a sharp look-out for the town bailiff. There they found the ugliest, wickedest, most pot-bellied of the town's merchants, one who had grown grey in cheating, calling out angrily:

'Tighten those girths. Lash those palm leaves over the water skin. We shall never get off tonight at this rate.'

'Where is old Ephraim going?' Fan asked a bystander.

'To Akaba. All across the wilderness of Sin to trade with the Gippos.' Fan went up to the merchant and greeted him with:

'What cheer, Ephraim. My sister and I would like to come down with you to Akaba.'

'Would you now? Come back at sunset. I'll think about it.'

When they returned, Ephraim promised to take them down to Akaba on riding camels and to give them the food for their journey. 'I'll look after you like my own daughters.'

Niss remembered that one of Ephraim's daughters was a filthy creature who sold charcoal in the market and thought that he was not promising much. But she discreetly kept the reflection to herself. 'What is old Ephraim getting out of it?' flashed across Fan's mind, but the unanswered question was soon forgotten.

They started that night and were soon out of the cultivated strips into the waste land and when the sun rose there was nothing in sight but a range of tall, pink mountains on the left, a plain stretching to the sea on the right and broken rocks and sands ahead. It was a prosperous journey. Every morning Fan and Niss would be among the first stirring and as soon as Ephraim gave the word they would ride ahead, one on each side of the guide who was a thin, bearded man of the desert with little eyes set on each side of a hawk nose. There were not many signs of life. Sometimes they would pass a ring of blackened stones where other travellers had camped – but there were no men.

Animals were few. Once a couple of ostriches raced before them and disappeared into the white glare; once they saw an oryx which they took to be a unicorn until it stopped and turned to face them and then they thought they saw that there were two horns nearly touching. At night they sometimes heard jackals and the yelp of the little desert foxes. And often there were the tiny footprints of Jerboas. But of the fiercer animals which they had met in the mountains they saw nothing. They were three weeks in the waste lands before they saw Akaba in a cleft of the sea between high mountains. The town they had come so far to see was a miserable collection of huts hidden among date palms. But there was a ship on the sea steering for the shore and two other ships with their bowsprits tied to date palms on the beach.

That night they were too tired and too disappointed in the miserable town to do anything but sleep. Next morning Ephraim came up to them with a smile on his fat lips and said they should go to the steam bath after their long journey: it would get the sand of the desert out of their heads and ease their saddle sores. He gave them a coin each and showed them where the hammam was built. Wondering what it would be like, they went there. A thin negress with no flesh on her long bones took charge of them. She stripped them naked, put them to sweat in a hole where red hot stones were thrown into a pool of water; then she put them side by side on a wooden bench, pummelled and slapped each of them in turn, sluiced them with cold fresh water and left them to cool off. Before she rubbed them dry she stopped to look at their bodies and said: 'Like as two almond kernels in one shell. If one man buys both of you he will think he is having the same girl every night.'

'Do you hear that?' asked Fan. Niss nodded. The negress went away and came back saying that Ephraim had sent them new linen smocks and that two of his men were waiting for them.

'Where are our own clothes?' asked Niss.

'I burned them in the boiler. They were too dirty to wash.'

So Fan and Niss came out of the hammam wearing fine white linen tunics. Ephraim and two of his men were waiting and walked along with them. But they were forewarned.

In the market were thin red-brown Egyptians and a group of girls standing in their best clothes with braided hair and waiting with downcast eyes.

'You see,' said Fan.

They watched a thick-lipped Babylonian walk up to a fuzzy-haired fat girl and say something to the thin Egyptian standing beside her. The Egyptian ordered her to stand up, to take off her smock, to turn round. All of which the girl did in a bored, lethargic way.

'The slave market,' said Niss.

'Now I know why Ephraim was so generous, mounting us on camels, giving us our food . . .' said Fan.

'Paying for us to be washed and made clean so that the buyer should not be put off by our sweaty carcases,' interrupted Niss.

'We'll give him a hot reception,' said Fan confidently.

'Look, that pitch might come in useful,' said Niss. For beside the market a sailor had been tarring the bottom of a boat turned upside down and had left a bucket full of pitch.

Ephraim came up with an elegant, slinky Egyptian with almond eyes, wearing a striped cotton kilt. His bare skin was oiled and perfumed; his black hair carefully waved.

'Pearls beyond price . . .' Ephraim was saying. The Egyptian without listening took Fan by the chin.

'Open widely . . . let's see those teeth,' he said.

Fan hesitated, smiled, opened her mouth widely and then as he leant forward to look at her teeth, spat full in his face. The Egyptian slave dealer was so astounded that he stepped back and his first action was to wipe his face. Only then did he raise his rhinoceros hide whip and hit Fan. But Niss had meanwhile seized the bucket of pitch and, as the man hit Fan, she brought it down over his head from behind. Men came running up. Someone pulled the bucket off the slave dealer who was blinded and unable to breathe. Another Egyptian cried: 'Beat them to death.'

'They are my property. No one marks their skins without paying me their price,' cried old Ephraim. 'Why, it's a trick to mark them and then buy them cheap. Just look what he's done to this girl.' And he pointed to the blood oozing from the weal on Fan's shoulder. Three Egyptians rounded on Ephraim.

'I'll teach you not to bring wild cats to market,' cried one hitting the old man across the face. Ephraim's servants, who had been standing beside Fan and Niss

[34]

guarding them, rushed to their master's defence and in a moment there was fight which grew to a riot. At the first moment when their guards left them, Fan and Niss ran. They could swim and they rushed into the sea, but finding they were not pursued they came ashore again and ran to the camels.

The camp was empty. They each hastily seized a water-skin and a sack of dates and mounted their camels and rode up the hillside, the way they had come. Half-way up the slope they stopped and looked back. There was a camel with a solitary rider coming after them.

'It's Ephraim,' said Fan.

They knew that together they were a match for the old man if it came to a fight. So when they had passed the crest, they let him overtake them.

'We must push on quickly,' said the old man. 'The punishment for brawling in Akaba is to have your right hand chopped off and hung round your neck.'

Niss laughed. 'We are due to be impaled too,' she said.

There was no pursuit. For a week they travelled through the desert with Ephraim, watching him closely and never both sleeping at the same time. Even when the old man lay fast asleep snoring, with his head on his saddle-bags, one or other would be sitting up to watch him. They often discussed why he offered them his food. Niss said that it was because they were useful to him. They collected dry camel dung in the evening for the fire and when they came to a well Fan would climb down to the bottom and fill the water skins with brackish water, which smelt but which was all there was to drink. But Fan thought that he still had plans of selling them if they fell in with any merchants travelling through the desert.

One evening sixteen days later when they had eaten a broth made with dried meat and some goat cheese, Niss who had the first watch, found that she could not keep awake. The fire got bigger and nearer and then went a long way off. She still had sense enough to be alarmed and she tried to wake Fan, but though she pulled at her arm and even dragged her along the ground, Fan would not wake up enough to understand what she said. Niss fell down, rolled over and lost consciousness. Next morning Fan woke up. The sun was high in the sky; Niss was asleep beside her and they were alone, Ephraim and the three camels had disappeared.

Fan got to her feet but she felt sick. Everything seemed to go round and round. She woke Niss, they moved into the shade of a rock and fell asleep again. It was evening when they woke up and it was only then that they fully understood what had happened to them. Ephraim had drugged them with opium or hashish when they ate the stew he gave them. Then he left them in the wilderness with nothing. No water; no food. On foot they could not overtake a man riding a camel and he had an eighteen hour start of them anyway. They could not hope to get back alive across the wilderness to Akaba, and if they did they would have their right hands struck off and be whipped to death afterwards. That was unimportant: it was far away. But they had no food and water and they were hungry and thirsty.

'Our only hope is to follow the tracks of the camels,' said Fan. Niss nodded. 'They will lead us eventually to another well, or something might fall off one of the pack animals without Ephraim noticing it.'

'What a hope,' said Niss.

They slept again and started directly it was light enough to see the tracks in the sand.

They had nothing with them except the linen smocks they had put on at the hammam. Ephraim had even taken Fan's leopard skin, which was an added cause for hatred, but which turned out to be lucky for her.

The sun rose and in an hour the flints under their bare feet were burning. The sun pressed on them like a hand of fire. The wind blew and the blown sand blinded them and there were no camel footprints left in the sand. Fan staggered on. Niss could go no further. She was parched; she had no will or strength. But just for a moment she looked up. Even at the point of death, the world was beautiful to her.

To her surprise she saw two swallows flying towards her. 'Fan,' she called, and Fan heard and stopped. The swallows flew up to them, twittering and hovering in

[37]

the air beside them, beating their little wings. Their throats were red and their backs and tails steel blue in the sunlight.

'If there are swallows there is water,' thought Fan and she turned and staggered for a few yards. And then her strength gave out, and she fell.

Suddenly there was a rush in the air and there were birds everywhere. Niss came to, with a pigeon beating its wings in front of her face and as she focused on it she saw it drop a little bunch of grapes from its bill. She put out her hand and they were real. She pressed them into her mouth and the juice ran over her stiff tongue. A minute later and there was the whistling of wings and the sound of fruit pattering on the sand beside her.

She looked to see what had happened to Fan and saw her sitting up only a few yards away cramming a pomegranate into her mouth. As soon as they had finished spitting out the seeds there was another rush of wings and dropping plums. A wild duck circled round them quacking loudly; then it alighted near them watching Fan with a wary eye. She made an unsuccessful grab at it and it flew off leaving an egg on the sand. Fan grabbed that, broke it and poured it down her throat. A moment later a goose alighted and soon flew off leaving an egg for Niss; she cracked it on a stone, swallowed it and laid her head on the sand.

In their sleep they were aware of angels' wings. They

did not know that as they lay under the burning sun upon the scorching sand that they were saved from death by a pair of pelicans who shaded them from the sun's rays by holding up their wings and that they were continually fanned by the wings of swallows and martins hovering anxiously.

During the night the weather changed. One by one the blazing planets faded, the sparkle of the cold and distant stars was blotted out by mists such as had not been seen in those desert lands since the third day when God parted the waters and the earth. Now the Old Fellow was preparing to stir them up again. The mists tempered the cold of the desert night and next morning the flaming sun was hidden and all was damp and fresh.

When Niss and Fan woke up they found fruit and eggs near them but not a bird in sight. They were alone once more, but the gifts were there to prove that they had not dreamed the miracle of the day before.

They found it easy going after they set off. The sun showed at intervals like a silver coin sliding out from the walls of mist and cloud. After they had walked for an hour or two they came to the edge of the high ground and passing between high rocks could see palm trees in the distant plain, so they knew that there must be water and that they were saved.

They sat down on the rocks and looked down into the plain.

Then just as Fan was saying: 'Well, we're safe

enough now,' Niss looked back the way they had come and made a sign for silence. Fan could see that her sister was in terror.

'Don't move,' whispered Niss. And Fan obediently sat motionless though she would dearly have liked to turn her head. And then she felt some creature breathing down her neck and she smelt a smell of meat and of a great warm beast. She leaped to her feet turning round as she did so to face whatever it might be. And there just behind where she had been sitting was a great lion with his lioness close beside him. Fan was turned to stone. And in her stony trance she heard Niss say:

'Good lion. Have you come to make friends?' And the lions, which had halted when Fan sprang up, stepped forward until they touched the two girls. They smelled the two sisters all over, and the lions' whiskers tickled Niss so that she shuddered a little and almost laughed, and then the lions yawned showing their enormous teeth and their rough tongues, and then sat down beside them. When Fan had recovered herself enough to touch the lion, she looked up and saw that animals were coming down everywhere from the hills. It was an army of wild animals of all sorts and sizes and shapes. Like an army, they came in ranks, perhaps because the edge of the high land formed a low cliff and there were only certain passages down which they could descend on to the lower ground and thus they were split into files. It was noticeable that the grass-eating animals kept away from the flesh-eaters, and that the small animals kept out of the way of the very big ones.

So looking back the way they had come, Fan and Niss saw a column with tigers, panthers, wild cats, lynxes, wolves and foxes, another column with stags, antelopes, goats, ibex, wild sheep, horses, donkeys, zebras, camels. Behind these and overtopping them, were two immense creatures which they had never seen before, picking their way with the utmost care lest they should slither and break their immense long yellow legs, which corresponded to their amazingly long necks. Niss, seeing that they were following a pair of dromedaries which they somewhat resembled, called them camelopards because they consorted with the camels and were spotted like the leopard. Her name stuck to them until very recently.

Another column was headed by two immense hippopotamuses followed by rhinoceroses of different colours, some with one horn and some with two. Behind them came all the pig tribe, bristling and tusked and looking about suspiciously with their small eyes.

Between other rocks down the declivity came the hares, rabbits, rats, mice, jerboas in such a multitudinous variety that the desert itself seemed to be in movement. On one side, keeping well apart were the lizards and all the restless, darting, rustling snakes.

All these were in files coming down separate paths from the plateau. But suddenly on the tallest, most impassable of the rocks which divided the paths of the grass-eaters and the flesh-eaters – suddenly on the very top of this rock a dark figure appeared and stood on its hind legs while it jabbered and beckoned to its companions behind. And suddenly the rock was covered with other monkeys; swarming with them, they came bounding, leaping, struggling up from the back with difficulty, pointing with their hands, and then, untroubled by the sheer precipice in front of them, formed themselves into a living chain and then, when all but a few had got down, waited with open arms to catch those who had to slither down the face of the rock or jump. It was a pantomime, acted from mere joy of life. The other beasts were stately and reserved, the monkeys were in wild spirits, chattering, laughing, howling, beating their breasts in mock terror, then turning cartwheels and somersaults for joy. Only when their path approached that of the snakes did they scamper off with cries of anxiety and rage.

Fan and Niss were still staring, as well they might, at this spectacle, when the lioness stood up and with her great paw twisted Fan about in her tracks and pushed her forward. It was a signal that they must start if they were to keep at the head of the army of animals. The lions strode forward untiring but the girls found it more than they could do to keep up. Seeing Fan covered in sweat and out of breath the lioness offered her her back to ride upon and when she saw her sister mounted, Niss climbed on the tigress just behind without waiting for an invitation. It had taken such a short time for them to know that all the animals were behaving for a special occasion and that they could trust them completely.

They found it delightful to be riding bareback and practically naked, for they had to pull up their smocks in order to ride astride. So they gripped the furry flanks with their bare thighs and calves, but even so riding needed balance. So, often, they had to grip the scruff to avoid falling off sideways.

The army of beasts came pouring down from the wilderness into the plain and so they came to the sown lands.

The people they caught sight of in the distance took one look and did not wait for their coming, and when at last they reached the town it seemed that already it was a city of the dead. All the doors were bolted and the shutters up and there was no life – no, not even a dog or a cat roaming in the streets.

But having arrived in the mountain village, the files of assorted animals had to wait and take their turns according to Noah's orders and the laws of precedence.

The flesh-eating animals came first, the great herbivores next, with the horses, asses, zebras taking precedence of the ruminants, the pig tribe and the small creatures pressed bravely forward being warm-blooded and so taking precedence of serpents and lizards. Last of all came the tortoises, bravely setting their best foot forward lest they be left behind.

Yet all did not go exactly as at a presentation at court. For sometimes Shem would call out: 'Halt those bears! We have a corner to fill up. Let's see – it would do fine for the beavers.'

And Noah would pick up his speaking trumpet and bellow:

'Beavers wanted. Beavers forward.' And after a long wait the unfortunate beavers would come paddling forward side by side and modestly make their way up the gangway, horrified at having so much attention given to them and then for their pains find themselves stowed away in some dark, noisome angle under the ship's ribs by Shem.

The monkeys alone had no sense of precedence and no shame. On reaching the town they had rushed in a crowd to perch on roof tops, to invade the temple, to throw pebbles into the top-storey windows of houses. Then when they reached the village and they saw the ark they made a rush for it, trying to get aboard before Noah was ready and out of turn at that. Noah had washed his head and beard and was wearing a white linen smock. He had parted his hair in the middle and his beard also and he was as calm and sober as the occasion demanded.

When the monkeys rushed forward he made a gesture to stop them and only two of the wretched creatures slipped past him unnoticed before Ham and Shem and Japheth, armed with pitchforks and shovels, turned them back.

[44]

'Monkeys last of all!' said Noah in a grim voice of authority, and what faces they made at him! And Fan and Niss realised that the animals understood what was said to them though they could not answer in human language.

'Lion and Lioness. Tiger and tigress,' Noah intoned solemnly.

Nobody noticed the two woolly monkeys which had climbed to the ridge of the Ark's roof and peered down with mocking wonder.

When Noah saw Fan riding astride the lioness, he cried out:

'Spawn of Satan! Away with you!' and Ham plucked Fan from her mount and threw her over the side of the gangplank. Luckily for her she landed in an orange tree – otherwise she might have broken her neck. 'There's another of them,' cried Shem, darting towards Niss, who seeing what had happened to Fan, slipped off the tigress and escaped into the garden below, where she soon joined her sister.

Fan was watching the wise animals lining up in pairs and solemnly marching up the gangway into the ark while Noah called out their names and Ham and Shem and Japheth directed them along the gangway to their stalls. The spectacle was so fascinating that for a bit they forgot about the need for doing something about their own future. For they had got to get into the Ark somehow. They might indeed have gone on watching until it was too late to do anything if it had not been for an unexpected interruption. There had been two slight hitches before that: Noah had ordered the animals to march in two by two – but this proved to be impossible in the case of the elephants and the hippopotamuses. The elephants obviously did not trust the gangway and would not venture on it until it had been cleared of all other creatures. The hippopotamuses barged along indifferent to whether it broke or not, their attitude implying: 'Whoever gets hurt, it won't be me.'

But the real hitch came with the arrival of the camelopards. They were as great a surprise to the builders of the ark, as they had been to Niss and Fan, and it was clear that with the best will in the world they could not get in, or be accommodated in any of the stalls.

'Halt!' cried Noah. And then looking up into the sky and cupping his hands to make his words carry; he shouted:

'Hold it, Oh Lord. Hold it. We shall need another three or four hours.' Then turning to Japheth, he said:

'They'll have to shake down with the elephants. But you must cut holes in the roof for their heads and rig some tarpaulins to cover them. I reckon you can cut the holes now, put them in and make all ship-shape with a sort of hencoop over their heads while we are shipping the rest of the cargo.'

[46]

'I think both necks could go through one hole. But what about feeding them?' asked Japheth.

'Well thought of,' said Noah. 'You'll have to fix it as you think best.'

'I think a trapdoor on one side of the ridge and a cradle on ropes with a pulley to take up the hay,' said Japheth.

'Good boy. Well, I'll knock off for a drink while Japheth cuts the hole and gets these animals in, whatever they are. Shem, I want you to take over for a bit. I'm whacked.' And Noah retired indoors.

Suddenly Niss said to Fan: 'You see. You heard what Noah said to God? The flood is coming in a few hours' time. We shall be drowned.'

'We must get aboard,' said Fan. They looked up at the ark and there on the ridge of the roof, getting in Japheth's way as he stood on the top of a ladder sawing a hole in the roof, were the two woolly monkeys.

'They weren't counted,' said Niss.

Fan gravely nodded her head up and down – a gesture which was very different from Niss's quick nod of assent.

'You mean,' she said, 'that we could go as them?'

'Stowaways,' said Niss. 'Once on board, it would be simple. But we must get in as them.'

'We must get disguises,' said Fan. 'What about lambskin?'

'Lambskin would do, except for the faces,' said Niss.

'The old saddler could make them,' said Fan.

They ran off and found him hiding in the cellar under his shop. Once they had explained that there was no danger from the serpents which were waiting their turn to go on board and infesting the pavement, he agreed to do a rush job for them. Luckily he had just bought a large batch of the skins of new-born lambs.

'It will be expensive. It will cost you half a gold dinar each. And when will you pay?'

'Tomorrow,' said Fan.

'Well, I wouldn't trust everyone,' he said, as he measured them, 'but I'll trust you.'

'We'll pay if you get the job done within four hours,' said Fan.

'I'll do my best,' said the saddler, taking a waxed thread out of his mouth. 'Come back in two hours.'

'Ha, ha!' laughed Fan directly they were outside.

'What a damned swindle,' said Niss. 'It seems awful that he should be drowned and that if our plan succeeds, we may escape.'

'Such is life,' said Fan very pleased with herself.

'You are a bloody-minded brute. I hate you,' said Niss.

'I'm not God. I'm not responsible for the flood – if there is going to be a flood,' replied Fan.

'I'm sure there is,' said Niss. 'Noah might be wrong, but not the animals.'

'Well, if there isn't, we shall have to pinch a gold

dinar from somewhere by tomorrow morning,' said Fan.

'I don't think it's fair,' said Niss.

'Oh, be your age. It's a gamble. He's taking a chance that we don't pay him for his work. We are taking a chance that he won't be drowned before we legally have to.'

'It's heads we win, tails he loses,' said Niss.

'I wish it were,' said Fan. 'Then I should know I had a head for business. But suppose Noah asks God to hold up the deluge for a couple of days? Suppose Shem spots that we aren't woolly monkeys? Why then we are cooked.'

Niss nodded.

They went back and Fan stripped and the old cobbler sewed her in to her new lambskin suit. He had cut a little mask of soft black leather for her face.

'Are you going to one of these fancy dress parties, my dear?' he asked.

'No. We are getting together with the animals,' said Niss.

'What a pair you are. Well, you look just like proper monkeys,' he said, as he finished sewing Niss into her suit.

The last stitches were in none too soon, for the snakes had disappeared and there was an unholy jabbering from the monkeys who were the last to go aboard.

Part Two

J U S T as the pair of new woolly monkeys came in sight of the ark, they saw Noah come to the top of the gangway. His face was very red and he swayed as he walked and held on to the rail with one hand. Fan and Niss had never seen a drunk man because in those days nobody made grapes into wine or barley into beer and distilling hadn't been invented, so there was no whisky, or brandy, or vodka, or saki, or slivovits to make glad the heart of man.

Noah was the first man to make wine and he was feeling very jovial and happy. All the animals were coming on board according to plan.

For a moment he looked at it all, then he said to Shem in a thick, blurry voice:

'Thank ye, me boy. I'll take over now.'

'I had better finish the job, hadn't I?' said Shem looking dubiously at his father.

'No, I'll take over. I've a few words to say to The Lord when I've got 'em all aboard.'

Shem smirked insolently and shrugged his shoulders, but he obeyed. He knew that, ridiculous though it seemed, the old man was listened to by The Lord and could talk to him almost as an equal. Fan and Niss pushed themselves in among the monkeys and went up the gangway side by side. Just as the pair in front reached Noah, Fan caught hold of the tail of the female monkey in front and pinched it. The monkey squealed and Noah was furious.

'If you can't behave like the other beasts, I'll have you slung off the ship. You pair, you'll stand and wait till I make up my mind whether to let you on board or not,' he said. 'Come on the rest of you.'

Fan and Niss went past gravely with downcast eyes.

'Why the hell can't you all behave like those pretty, pretty ickle woolly monkeys? Sweet little things,' said Noah sentimentally. 'Not like you ugly, indecent blue-arsed mandrils,' he added, looking at the next pair. 'Why, I wouldn't have any of you aboard if it weren't part of my bargain with The Lord. I would take those woolly monkeys though.'

Naturally the monkeys who knew well enough that Fan and Niss were imposters were beside themselves with rage. But they did not dare show it, though as soon as they were safely aboard, they would have stripped the twins of their disguises if they had not escaped into the snake pit.

As it was, Fan had her finger bitten and Niss a pinch in the bottom which she felt for a week.

The snakes were unfriendly, obviously resenting the invasion, as well they might, as it was almost impossible to put a foot to the ground without treading on them. There was some hissing; a cobra put up its hood and one of the rattlesnakes rattled. Fan and Niss got out as quickly as they could and by good fortune found themselves in the large cattery where they were welcomed with a waving of tails and the friendliest of growls and purrs on all sides. But before they could settle down, there was a tremendous shout from Noah obviously directed into the sky.

'All aboard, Oh Lord! You can let her rip now!'

A blinding flash of lightning followed his words and the peals of thunder which came after went on and on. During the next flash Fan saw that the snow leopard was crouching at her feet in terror with his ears back and his claws sunk in the cedar deck. She knelt beside him, put her hand on the beast's head and said: 'Steady now. It's all O.K.'

In the same brief flash Niss had seen that she was standing between the two tigers and that they were desperate and bewildered.

She put one arm round the tiger's neck and one round that of the tigress. 'It's all right, darlings. We are all in the same boat. It's sink or swim for all of us.' In each case Fan and Niss found that their words seemed to reassure and comfort the animals. And at that moment down came the rain.

The two sisters were worn out by all their adventures and as soon as the beasts were calm they fell asleep on the straw between the great cats which had befriended them. When they woke the deafening drumming of the rain on the roof continued but there was an added sibilance for all around it was falling now not on land but into a shallow sheet of water. And there was also the roar of torrents pouring off the sides of the mountains. When they looked out later they saw that the ark was still firmly aground – and she remained so for three days, for she drew fifteen feet of water. During those days there was a tremendous current swirling past. All the water off the mountains was pouring down the valley and on its way engulfing the town five feet deep. This was lucky for those on board, as none of the townspeople could get near to the ark and attempt to find refuge upon it. After the third day the current slowed up and the water began backing up the valley.

Then in the middle of the fourth night Fan and Niss woke suddenly, for the ark had tilted. One end had risen in the water while the other was still stuck fast so that the deck on which they were lying was at an angle and their feet were a little higher than their heads. They lay silent, each suddenly aware of the big furry wild beasts around them.

Two hours later the ark made another sharp movement and the deck levelled. Both ends were afloat. It was the moment they had excitedly been waiting for, but the sound of the rain numbed them, they felt no urge to get up to look out into the darkness. As they dozed off they felt the ark swing round and then suddenly were brought wide awake: the ark had bumped into a tree, or a rock.

Niss was frightened; everything seemed very dangerous and was extremely strange. She put out her hand and touched the rough scruff of the tiger and then felt the creature on the other side of her stirring, and then the rough tongue of the tigress passed over her hair and her shoulder. And then just because it was all friendly as well as strange, she fell asleep.

They did not wake until the morning when Japheth came with a lantern, but he waited to show a light to Ham who brought a barrow load of meat to push through the bars. Owing to the darkness – there were few windows in the ark and most of those were kept closely shuttered – and to the leaden sky outside and to the stirring excitement of the animals waiting their turn to be fed, Fan and Niss were able to crouch undetected in a pile of straw at the back of the big loose box – for that is all the big cattery was. The animals were fed by precedence: Japheth began with the lions well before dawn, and it was dark again before the monkeys got their coconuts – a grievance which they exploited to the full.

The lizards, snakes and tortoises were not fed at all for the whole five months they were on board. The bears had sensibly hibernated and so did all sorts of other creatures: the dormice, squirrels and bats and badgers. But the great majority was shockingly underfed and rapidly lost condition in consequence.

It looked as though God – or Noah acting on instructions – had miscalculated about the quantities of fodder required. To feed himself, his family and all the carnivorous animals, Noah had allowed for five of each domestic animal to be slaughtered on the voyage. For they had been taken aboard by sevens, whilst of the wild creatures a pair had sufficed. Thus two domestic animals were for repopulating the flocks and herds which man required and five were slaughtered during the voyage. The meat supplies consisted therefore of one ox, one buffalo, one sheep, one goat, one camel, one dromedary, one horse, one ass, one pig and one tame rabbit per month. Also one of every species of domestic fowl and waterfowl. It may be that God had intended Noah to ship seven elephants instead of a pair. But he had not planned the ark to hold them and indeed the tonnage of hay needed would have been greater than the forage merchants of Palestine and Syria could have supplied. But whoever was to blame, the animals, especially the small carnivores – such as stoats and weasels were famished, and though they were áll bound by God to be of good behaviour, the strain on their tempers was terrible, particularly as they were living at close quarters with their natural prey. One result was that during the later part of the voyage they became far noisier. At first there was only the chattering of monkeys – and that was subdued by the noise of the rain and by its depressing influence. But after the rain

[58]

stopped and spirits rose, there was an incessant barking of dogs, howling of wolves, whickering of ferrets, mewing of cats, bellowing of cattle and baaing of sheep.

'The hungry sheep look up and are not fed.' But if they were not fed they were at all events exalted.

On the evening of the first sabbath after the rain began, Noah called his family together and addressed them in these words:

'God's promises have come to pass and all of us who have listened to His words have not laboured in vain for all these twenty years. But let not any of you think that we have been permitted to build this ark to save our own miserable lives. It is only by the grace and goodness of The Lord that we are permitted to be here.

'In the Beginning God made man in His own image. But when He saw how this reflected image of Glory chose to live, when He perceived that sin and beastliness, cowardice and cruelty, meanness and self-seeking had been attached by man forever to His Divine Image, then He grew wroth and thought that He would do away with man as man does with a litter of unwanted kittens. So He decreed the Deluge. But then, in His goodness He bethought Him of all the lovely birds and beasts that He had created. He looked at them and saw that they were beautiful and that man's works were not. So He decided that they must be saved. Therefore He commanded me, His servant, to build

[59]

this ark so that those that were beautiful should not perish. And because you and I have laboured for The Lord He has allowed us to live so that we might tend the beasts of the field and the birds of the air and be their servants. But we are not saved for our own sakes, but for theirs. The meanest rat or frog or moth is more precious in the eye of The Lord than man or woman. Only if we serve the beasts humbly and live for them rather than for ourselves, shall we be saved alive. So to all of you I say: Bear yourself lowly. Be meeker than the conies among the rocks if you seek the favour of The Lord. And without His favour you are utterly lost.'

But praise was not food: consideration yielded no calories. Fan and Niss suffered from hunger as much as any of the creatures aboard. Debarred by the enmity of the monkeys from claiming their share of nuts, they depended for some time almost entirely upon the marrow which they pushed out of the bones with a stick after the lions, tigers and panthers had finished with them. They might perhaps have died early in the voyage if the she-wolf had not had a litter. Her cubs were immediately taken away and drowned on Noah's order, for breeding had been forbidden while in the ark. Fan and Niss took the place of the cubs, thus antedating Romulus and Remus by nearly 1,600 years. It is probable indeed that that famous pair of twins would not have survived to build Rome had not the ancestress of all mother wolves passed on the tradition of suckling human babies when bereaved of her own cubs.

This has been the practice among the wolves of India, a country where all men and beasts are more ruled by tradition than in any other part of the world.

It was there that Mowgli was suckled and all the wolf children who have been brought from the freedom of the jungle into captivity as well as hundreds who have spent their lives running with the wolf packs and who have given rise to the legends of were-wolves.

When Fan and Niss were at their hungriest, scavenging for marrow bones in the lions' den, a sudden quarrel broke out between them. Fan, who was quick and ruthless had seized three bones and as the old lion turned indifferently away from a fourth, she grabbed at it. Niss put out her foot, tripped Fan and sent her flying and the three bones she was holding under her arm scattered in all directions. Niss got the lion's bone and one of the fallen ones.

'Give that back,' said Fan when she had picked herself up and then picked up the other two bones. 'Hand it over, it's mine.'

'You have no right to it,' said Niss.

'Hand it over,' repeated Fan.

'You've got two. I've got two. Share and share alike,' said Niss.

'I'll bash you, you thief, you low cur, tripping me

[61]

up,' said Fan, and swung the largest of the bones she was holding.

' It's like you to be a greedy hog,' said Niss.

Fan flew at her sister and each struck and hit the other with the bones in their hands. Blood flowed from Niss's temple and Fan's cheek and they collapsed in a heap wrestling on the floor. After a few moments they broke away and Fan, who was first on her feet, was about to hit Niss again when she was grabbed by the neck from behind. Niss, rising, saw with horror that Fan was being held in the lioness's jaws. In a flash it occurred to her that it was because Fan was bleeding; the lioness had smelled blood. She was about to throw herself at the animal to rescue her sister, when she was knocked backwards and the old lion put his paw on her chest.

Each of the sisters lay absolutely still for some little while. How long they could not tell, for every second seemed an age. Niss, looking up into the great yellow eyes and the tawny mane of the old lion was the first to recover herself.

She saw that she was just being held down and that he was not going to kill and eat her and she said:

' I'm sorry. I won't fight any more. Let me go.'

The lion held her firmly, but he looked across at his mate.

' Fan, tell her we won't fight any more,' called Niss.

' All right. It's all over. We won't fight if you let us go,' said Fan.

[62]

The lioness released her and the old lion lifted his great paw from Niss's chest. She got up and found herself shaking so she could scarcely stand. She was feeling sick. Fan was holding her neck and trying to twist her head. But every new position hurt worse. Without giving a thought to the bones they climbed out of the lion's den and went away in silence to the hayloft. It was some time before either of them spoke and then it was not to discuss what had just happened.

'I have often wished we were one person and not two. But actually as things have turned out we are damned lucky to be twins,' said Fan.

'How so?' asked Niss in a supercilious tone which would ordinarily have infuriated Fan. But she took no notice, because she was explaining the thought which had just come to her.

'If we hadn't been two, we should never have got into the ark. We had to be a pair to be let in. If we were one person we should have been drowned long before now.'

'That's true,' said Niss nodding her head. 'That makes up for a lot.'

'Crumbs, I am hungry,' said Fan. 'And I can't seem to get my head straight on my neck.'

The rain fell in an almost solid mass – without pause or alteration and the sound of it beating on the roof of the ark never ceased and added to the depression of the company.

Niss and Fan being reasoning creatures who knew

[63]

good from evil, or at least had ideas on the subject, soon found themselves discussing the rights and wrongs of the Deluge.

Niss started it by the words: 'It can't be right.'

Fan snorted. 'Right! There is no right about it. He has just drowned the entire population of the globe – except for present company. Millions of happy and innocent people.'

'He has saved Noah and his family. That is to His credit,' said Niss.

'But He has drowned the saddler who was as kind a man as you could find anywhere,' said Fan.

'And whom you swindled of a gold dinar.'

'What has that to do with it?'

There was a silence while Niss thought about it.

'I suppose if He can hear what Noah says, He can hear you,' she said at last.

'Actually Noah always shouts at Him as though He were a very long way off. But I jolly well hope He can hear me,' said Fan. 'I'm not muzzled. And if you want to know, I *despise* Him for the Deluge.'

Niss nodded her head. 'Yes, I'm with you there. In any case He wouldn't like one just because one was afraid of Him.'

'I'm not sure of that. According to Noah, God drowned the world because mankind had become corrupt. I suspect it is the other way round. Power corrupts. Absolute power corrupts absolutely.'

[64]

'So you think that He just drowned everyone in a fit of temper and decided to make a fresh start?'

'That is the theory – if He exists.'

'Oh, come off it. This ark full of animals is proof enough that He exists.'

'I don't feel sure,' said Fan. 'Noah might be the most marvellous weather prophet ever known. Or he may have discovered how to make it rain like the African witch doctors.'

'I wish he could discover how to make it stop,' said Niss. 'But how do you account for the animals coming and for their behaviour?'

'I don't know. Hypnotism possibly. I don't begin to know enough to have an opinion. But I shall try my best to find out. At present, just because we are ignorant and can't be bothered to think it out, we father it all on God.'

'You admit it's all a bit odd,' said Niss.

'I grant you that. Couldn't be odder,' said Fan cheerfully. 'All the same you'll agree that if it's God's plan, it's a pretty foul show.'

'Foul beyond belief,' said Niss.

'That's what makes me suspect that Noah thought it up. It's typical human behaviour.'

'What's Noah getting out of it?'

'Everything. An obscure drunkard in a hick town in Palestine whom everyone laughed at, has his revenge on his neighbours, and becomes the sole progenitor of the world to be. You can't beat that.'

The ark was appallingly overcrowded and the animals, among whom Fan and Niss were classed, had nothing whatever to do and no chance of exercise. Noah and his family – at least his wife, sons and daughters-in-law, led busy lives. Every moment was occupied in cutting trusses of hay, slaughtering a sheep or some other beast, skinning them, and in feeding and watering the animals.

The latter task took three hours every morning. The ark had no pumps – for they had not been invented, and Noah and his sons had not thought to put a cistern in the roof to catch the rain. So Japheth rigged four little platforms with companion ladders leading down to the water, one on each side at each end of the vessel. (We must call them ends since the ark had neither prow nor stern.) From the nearest of these to the stalls to be watered, Japheth or his brothers would descend and fill a couple of buckets. These companion ladders proved very useful later on to Niss and Fan. And it was from one of these that the women drew water.

Mrs Noah and her daughters-in-law found it almost impossible to do the washing. It was easy to wash a shirt, but impossible to get it dry. As there was only one fireplace in the ark, laundry could not be dried in front of the fire, which was needed for cooking.

This would not have mattered in fine weather. If the sun had been shining Noah's sons would have worked stripped to the waist. But as it was they had to wear clothes and they got soaked to the skin several

[66]

times a day. And each time they wanted to change into dry garments. So the women squabbled and got in each other's way and Mrs Ham actually went and complained to Noah and said that she would never have come on the cruise if she had known that it was going to be one long washing day all the week. Noah heard her out in patient silence, then without replying, he put his beard in his mouth and went out into the rain where she would not follow him.

But though Noah's sons and daughters-in-law had to work their fingers to the bone, there were some members of the family aboard who did no work at all. These were Noah's grandchildren, of whom the eldest were three boys, Gomer, Mizraim and Canaan, the two eldest of whom had thrown stones at the sisters and been rescued by Fan from the town boys at the puppet theatre. Gomer was Japheth's son and, like his father, was tall, fair and blue-eyed. Mizraim was Ham's son, and like all Ham's children took after his mother and was brown-skinned with dark eyes and short curly black hair. Besides the two older boys there was Canaan, Mizraim's brother, two sisters of Gomer's, two daughters of Shem's. Canaan and the girls were all much younger. By Noah's orders they were all kept in the forward hold which was mostly below the water line. It had been totally dark until Japheth had put in two portholes high up on the wall and out of reach.

When The Lord had commanded Noah to build the

ark twenty years before so as to save the animal creation from destruction. He had agreed to spare Noah, his wife and his three sons from the general fate of mankind. Noah had stipulated that if his sons should marry, their wives should be spared also, and the Lord had rather reluctantly agreed. Noah's imagination had not then envisaged that grandchildren might be born before the Deluge. He had no idea that the ark would take so long to build. When the time came to embark, Noah was afraid of raising the subject of whether the children should be saved or not. He knew The Lord well enough to know that if He were in one of His moods, He would not go an inch beyond the letter of their agreement. So it would be better to hide them somewhere in the ark where God was unlikely to notice them, than to risk His refusal which would lead to a mutiny among the crew and bring the whole project of saving the land animals to nothing.

After telling Japheth to make a nursery out of the forward hold, Noah pretended to know nothing about their being there. He became unreasonably annoyed whenever Japheth or Ham suggested that one of the boys ought to be made to do something useful, usually stumping off without saying anything. But if he were driven into a corner he would say:

'I don't think that The Lord would like it. It was understood that you and your brothers were to do all the work. Keep them out of sight.'

The Old Man's orders were obeyed when he was

[68]

around, but when he wasn't looking, taking his siesta, or sleeping off the second bottle, the mothers brought the little girls out for an airing. They were always grumbling that it was cruel to keep the little dears shut up all the time in a dark hold. If The Lord were looking when Noah was not, He must have thought it better to turn a blind eye on them.

But keeping Gomer and Mizraim shut up was far more difficult than doing the same with their little sisters. They were always escaping. But the second or third time that Mizraim did this, he was seen by Noah, chased by his orders and broke his leg jumping from the top bulwarks to the lower deck. After that he was laid up for nearly the whole of the time they were afloat.

But Japheth let his son out of the hold provided that he never let his grandfather see him. Gomer's idea of keeping out of sight was to wander along the alleyways between the cages and to prod the animals with a stick. Fan and Niss caught him doing this one afternoon. He was prodding the leopard which shut its eyes and snarled, but refused to give way, nor did he try to reach Gomer with a paw between the bars which he could have done.

'Let's stop that,' said Niss. Fan said nothing but went up behind Gomer quickly and caught him by the collar and the seat of his pants and lifted him off the ground. Niss snatched away his stick and vaulted over the bars beside the leopard and while Fan held him firmly against the barrier, Niss made as though to poke him in the face.

'You mayn't do that,' said Gomer. 'You are only a monkey, I'm a man.'

'You're a great oaf,' said Niss, and poked him very hard in the ribs. He squealed and then began to blubber and sob with pain. 'That was just to show you,' said Niss. 'I shall do it again if I have to, but not if you behave, because I don't like being cruel even to beastly boys.'

Gomer listened to the monkey talking with astonishment, but he pulled himself together and replied:

'I'm not a nasty boy. The Lord has drowned all the bad boys, but He hasn't drowned me because He loves me.'

Fan burst out laughing though she kept a tight grip on the collar of his coat.

'You bet your sweet life He does. Do you know why you are really alive? First because God doesn't even know that you are on board. If He did He would have you slung over the side to drown. But apart from that you are only alive because God loves animals. He intended to drown mankind and save the animals. But as animals can't build ships He made a bargain with your Grandad that if he would build an ark and save a pair of each of the beautiful innocent beasts, He would spare him and his family.'

Gomer listened in silence. He was very much impressed. He knew that the monkey was telling the truth and perhaps The Lord had put the words into its mouth.

'If you want The Lord to love you, make friends with the animals and love them,' said Niss.

'My Grandpa keeps saying that but I don't know how,' said Gomer, who stopped blubbering but kept rubbing the place where Niss had poked him hard.

'Go and ask that leopard's pardon,' said Fan.

'Oh, not the one I was touching up. Oh, please, I dare not.'

'You'll find it's easy,' said Fan, swinging the trembling boy over the barrier to Niss, who took him by the hand and led him to the leopard.

'He's sorry,' she said. 'He won't do it again.' But there was something forbidding in the leopard's eyes and Niss thought it better not to stay there. 'Let's start with the lion,' she said.

'I'm sorry, lion,' said Gomer. 'I won't touch up any of the animals again. I want to be friends. But I don't seem to know how.'

The lion looked at Gomer and what the boy saw there made him run for the barrier. Niss let him scramble over it. Fan caught him again by the collar. 'They don't believe in you,' she said.

'Honest, I'll never touch them up again.'

'Well, come along then. We'll try with the wild ponies and the zebras. They may like you better.'

They did. The little mare snuffled and though at first she pretended to bite, she allowed Fan to help Gomer to mount her. There was not room in the stall for her to do more than wheel round and round and push past the stallion, but Gomer was thrilled and full of happiness. 'You're the goods,' he said. 'You're the most smashing pony in the world.' At these words the pony stallion whinnied jealously but they pleased the mare who arched her neck with pride.

After Gomer had slid off the mare he put an arm round her neck and rubbed her muzzle and turned to Niss and Fan and said: 'I'm ever so grateful, you funny woolly monkeys, even though you did stick me so beastly hard in the stomach. I bet you marked me for life. See you again soon.'

The twins were pleased with what they had done, but Fan said: 'We shall have to keep out of his way or he will rumble us.'

The hay loft filled one end of the ark from deck level to roof. The remainder of the roof was a vast aviary in which serried ranks of torpid birds perched on the tie beams and on hundreds of rods placed between them as perches. It was always half dark and most of the birds were asleep, but there was a twittering just audible through the monotonous drumming of the rain just above one's head. At long intervals there were unexpected screams from the peacock or the macaws, but except at feeding time it was quieter than would have been expected. That is to say during the forty days of rain.

The little birds sat immobile through the long days

and nights conserving their vitality as best they might. Only the swallows skimmed from end to end in the twilight space, catching the flies which wandered in from the animals' loose boxes below. At the further end were the larger birds. The peacock and the Jungle Fowl perched high up so as to let their trains hang down undamaged; there was a row of gloomy eagles and vultures. Below, perched on the floor were all the storks, herons, egrets, ibis, flamingoes and other long-legged waders. In all this company only the owls were active and at home, pouncing on any of the illegitimate mice and rats that infested the grain store, or came scavenging after dropped bird seed.

Once every two or three days Mrs Japheth came up into the aviary. She let in some light, filled up the drinking troughs and scattered grain for the gallinaceous birds and finches and a sack of meal-worms and dried ants' eggs for the insect eaters and then a basket full of chopped-up lites for the eagles, hawks and vultures and dried sprats for herons and flamingoes. The geese and swans, needing fresh grass were often hungry, for the grain Mrs Japheth spared them was barely sufficient to keep them alive. It was a mistake to have brought them into the ark as those who had been left behind rode out the flood, as did all the ducks, seagulls, albatrosses and other sea birds.

Some of the little birds soon attached themselves to Niss and after she had made a few visits to the aviary, they would swoop upon her from their perches, covering her head and shoulders and her arms and taking crumbs between her lips from a piece of bread she held in her teeth.

Fan at the other end of the aviary made friends with the swan and with the raven, birds with which she and the successors of her way of thinking, maintained an association for many hundreds of years. The swans, like the geese, should not have been in the ark at all, and like the geese were on short commons.

Fan managed to steal grain for the swans, and some rotting scraps of meat from the lion cage, which she conveyed to the ravens. Like all parts of the ark, the smell of the aviary was disgusting though it had its own peculiar quality. Whereas everywhere else the humidity was such that a crust of bread turned green in a few hours, in the aviary the foul air was dry and stuffy and full of the scurfy powder of birds' quills. After every visit, Niss and Fan were white with birds' droppings. But in spite of these drawbacks they continued to visit the aviary two or three times a week. No one went there except Mrs Japheth on feeding days, so they were safe from detection. And the sisters had never forgotten that in the desert, they had owed their lives to the birds. They tried to repay them as best they could in the gloomy surroundings of the ark.

The ark had not been afloat a week before the stench down the alley-ways between the cages became so appalling that the twins had to give up sleeping in the large cat house.

It was the safest hide-out, but they thought breathing the foul air would bring on some fever. So before the doors were bolted for the night, they stole away into the hay-loft where they could sleep in comfort. There was far less noise there – only the elephants in their stall beside them clinking the chains on their ankles from time to time.

In spite of the stench, they managed to pass the day in the animals' cages. This was partly because there was nowhere else to go. It was forced upon them if they were to eat at all for they were still chiefly dependent upon the marrow from the bones given to the lions and tigers. But it was in fact slightly more tolerable in the cages during the day, as the doors of the alley-ways were left open so that there was some ventilation.

About the thirtieth night after the rains started Niss woke up in the hayloft to find herself held fast by wrists and ankles. Some creature was breathing into her face. From the smell she realised that she was lying in the dark in the power of monkeys. Nothing she could do could shake off the grip which held her and she wondered whether it were a gorilla. It was. She knew from the rustling that there were other monkeys near. She nearly shouted to Fan for help and then reflected that if the monkeys had not found Fan, she might escape. It would be better to keep silent and endure her fate. A little later the sound of struggling showed that Fan was also in the monkeys' power.

Not long afterwards she had no thought to spare for

her sister. For a hand tore off her mask and a wrinkled paw was passed over her face. She tried to bite it, but got her nose pulled. Then a paw was thrust down the neck of her disguise into the groove between her breasts, and then she was suddenly almost strangled as the sheepskin was pulled until it ripped open. The monkey was in no hurry. It tore at the sheepskin, pulled it off her shoulders and then went away. When it came back some minutes later it tickled her under one arm and then savagely tore the sheepskin off the arm with such force that she thought her elbow would be dislocated. Then it very carefully felt round each of her breasts and jabbered a little, perhaps with surprise. Suddenly she knew that another monkey was there which made four of them in all, counting the two which held her. The new monkey got hold of the sheepskin and tore it off her body. Niss was by this time so faint with fear that she was hardly conscious, but she knew that the two monkeys went away.

After a long time they came back and pulled the sheepskin off her legs. And suddenly the grip on her wrists and ankles was relaxed and they had let her go. She lay bathed in sweat and streaked with blood where they had scratched and bruised her and was almost fainting. She knew she was going to be sick but hadn't the strength to kneel, but made a little hole in the hay, was sick in it and lay back. There was a chuckle as the monkeys went away.

'Where are you, Niss?' came Fan's voice faintly.

She made a sound and not long afterwards a limp, exhausted figure flung herself into the hay beside her.

'Not on that side. I've been sick there,' she managed to say.

For a long time they lay without the strength to speak or think, only longing to forget the horrible feeling of the monkeys pawing their bodies while they were held immovable.

At last Fan said quietly: 'It slobbered over me.'

Daylight came and they hid in the furthest corner while Ham fetched forks full of hay for the elephants. The monkeys had left them stark naked.

'What are we to do?' asked Niss at last.

'I know what I'm going to do,' said Fan. 'I'm going out on deck into the rain to wash off the stink of those filthy baboons.'

They waited until the men had all gone to the other end of the ark and then stepped out on to the deck into the rain.

It came down on their bodies like steel rods, driving the breath out of their lungs. In a moment their heads were clean: their hair beaten like snakes on their shoulders, their bodies clean, the last taint of monkey and sweat and blood washed from them. They looked at each other's naked bodies with delight. It was so long that they had masqueraded as monkeys – now they were proud to be human. Their eyes sparkled. But they could not speak until they stepped back into the shelter of the eaves of the ark's roof.

'Gosh, but you're beautiful, Fan,' said Niss.

'I daresay you're not too bad. Your hair looks like snakes.'

Niss opened her mouth wide.

'Snakes! Why, we are saved!' Fan stared at her. 'Don't you see,' explained Niss. 'Just go to the snake pit and borrow a couple of the most venomous ones there. No monkey will ever come near us – or man either for that matter.'

'Wonderful,' said Fan.

'We will wear them round our necks,' said Niss.

'I suppose they'll play?' said Fan.

'Of course they will. Snakes like milk. We'll give them a little wolf's milk.'

'They weren't very friendly that time we went into the pit,' said Fan.

'That's because we were disguised as monkeys. And we trod on some of them too.'

They waited until they were dry and went to the snake pit where nobody was likely to see them as the snakes were never fed. The snakes seemed lethargic. They did not bother to hiss at them. Niss picked out an asp and Fan took a Russell's viper. The snakes looked at them with hard uncomprehending eyes. If they, the twins, had not been so full of their idea, they would have felt afraid of them. But without a thought of fear they wound them round their heads. Curiously enough the snakes liked the warmth of their bodies and livened up and presently allowed themselves to be made into collars.

'We had better live in the snake pit until we can find new disguises,' said Niss.

'Why have disguises at all?' asked Fan. 'I vote we brave it out. I'm sick of being a woolly monkey. I would rather be what I am.'

Niss said nothing. She was thinking.

'We'll have to make ourselves some grass skirts, or goatskin trousers or something, I suppose,' Fan went on.

'We can't dress entirely in snakes,' said Niss regretfully.

They caressed their snakes and enjoyed the feeling of strength when the snake wriggled ecstatically, and stiffened and moved again.

'We shall have to find something to wear at once,' said Niss.

'Better get that boy to lend us some of his clothes till we can make our own,' said Fan.

'You ask him,' said Niss who felt shy about being seen naked by Gomer. 'He'll be surprised to find we weren't woolly monkeys after all.'

'I wouldn't be a woolly, or any other kind of monkey ever again,' said Niss.

'I'm with you there. But I wouldn't mind being a wolf,' said Fan. 'Or a snow leopard. I should like that better because I don't want to be one of a pack.'

They waited in the snake pit until Noah's family

had assembled for their midday meal. Then directly they had heard Noah bellow out a Grace loud enough for The Lord to hear, they ran to the pony's loose box and climbed in and hid behind the pony and the stallion. An hour later Gomer sauntered up as they had expected. He stood by the bars and held out a piece of bread for the little mare on the flat palm of his hand and Niss thought she had never seen a more charming expression on anybody's face.

'Hullo, Gomer,' said Fan, standing up on the far side of the pony mare. Gomer stared unbelievingly at her.

'Who the devil are you?' he asked, but she could see that he knew the answer. 'You were one of the woolly monkeys, weren't you?'

'Yes, but we've had a bit of bad luck since we saw you last.'

'Oh?'

'The real monkeys caught us asleep and pulled our disguises off.'

Gomer laughed and laughed and beat his hands on his knees with delight. Fan had to wait until he was calm before she explained:

'So we need your help. We want you to lend us a couple of your shirts and two pairs of trousers.'

'There isn't anything on board to make you new disguises,' said Gomer.

'We aren't going to be disguised any more,' said Niss, popping up her head.

'They'll sling you overboard if they catch you,' said Gomer.

'I don't think they will,' said Fan. 'Now cut along and bring us some clothes. We'll let you have them back as soon as we can make ourselves some new ones.'

A few minutes later Gomer came back with two old shirts and two pairs of jeans.

'These are Mizraim's things. He don't want them. He's laid up. He jumped off the top bulwark and broke his leg. Let's have a look at you,' he said with a teasing smile of self-satisfaction. Fan beckoned him towards her but just as he put out an arm to pull her close, she pointed to the Russell's viper coiled round her neck. He dropped the shirts and jeans and ran. The sisters had scarcely finished dressing and laughing before Gomer was back, but he kept his distance.

'I guess you're evil spirits. Witches. It's all baloney about the monkeys stripping you, isn't it?' They laughed at him until they saw he was becoming uncomfortable.

'No, we got aboard disguised as woolly monkeys after they wouldn't let me come on board riding a lion and Niss riding a tiger.'

'Yes, I remember. But that doesn't prove you are not evil spirits. Why have you got the snakes, if you are human?'

'We've got these snakes so that the monkeys won't play any more tricks on us,' said Fan.

'And so Ham shouldn't try to throw us overboard

if we get caught,' said Niss. 'But if you will be our friend, we shall be ever so grateful.'

'I would like to be your boy friend. Only I don't much fancy that snake of yours.'

'He won't hurt you. Come and stroke him.'

'I dare not.'

Niss took hold of Gomer's hand and then taking the asp from round her neck, she let it slide over Gomer's arm and back into her bosom. They boy turned pale with fear, but he did not snatch his hand away or flinch and no harm resulted.

From that time Niss and Gomer became particular friends.

While the rain lasted Fan and Niss spent the greater part of the day asleep in one of their haunts – the snake pit was a favourite – only coming out in the evening when they met Gomer in the hay loft or the ponies' stall where he brought them a basket of food pilfered from Noah's table. It was wonderful to eat bread again. Sometimes there was a cake and once Gomer stole a pot of his grandfather's wine. There was also salt beef, ham and hard cheese. Noah's family had laid in plenty of provisions for the voyage for themselves. It was only the animals that went hungry in the ark and as soon as Fan and Niss had resumed human form they discovered the difference.

Just about midnight on the fortieth day after they had gone into the ark, the twins woke up. There was no sound of drumming rain on the roof above them.

It had stopped. They whispered to each other excitedly, climbed out of their nests of hay and went out to see. The sky was clear, a very dark blue and blazing with stars. The ark was riding peacefully on the waters. There was not a breath of wind. The darkness was fortunate for them for they nearly blundered into Noah. Indeed, they would have done so if they had not heard him muttering as he came towards them.

'All the wicked drowned. I shall never see one of them again. Safe down at the bottom of the water.' Those were all the words they could distinguish. Hearing the muttering, they drew back into the embrasure of the door which opened on to the deck and the words they caught were uttered as Noah went by them, tottering along the deck unsteadily. When he had gone they gave a quick look at the stars and went thankfully back to the hayloft where they slept until long after dawn the next day.

It was a glorious morning: the sun shone brilliantly in a blue sky.

The sisters decided to risk going out for a moment on deck.

'All the Noahs are on the sunny side of the ark. Listen, you can hear the women giving directions to the men about fixing up a clothes line. It is the first thing those miserable women would think of.'

'Yes, I think we shall be safe enough if we go out on the shady side,' said Fan. They looked up at the sky.

'How wonderful it would be to have a swim! I

[83]

haven't had a proper wash since we went to that hammam bath in Akaba,' said Niss.

They looked over the gunwale into the dark water, shadowy below them.

'Look! What's that?' exclaimed Fan in tones of doubt. 'It can't be . . . yes, it is!'

'Ugh! I shall be sick!' said Niss. And not long afterwards she was – but not till Fan and she had made out not one floating corpse, but dozens.

It is usual to speak of the drowned as 'food for fishes', and so no doubt they are in normal circumstances. But unlike the land animals which had accepted the hospitality of the ark, the fishes had been provided with far more food than they could cope with. Thus the corpses which floated round the ark had only suffered the effects of decomposition. They had not been nibbled. The remnants of their clothes indicated their sex and withered old people could be readily distinguished from those in the prime of life. Many were children. All of them were blown up with gas from the effects of decomposition. From their number the ark must have been floating over the site of a sizeable city – and the fortunate survivors were soon reminded of the fate of its inhabitants, for the smell of the rotting corpses was appalling.

'My God! And to think that we have to drink that water,' exclaimed Fan. And it was then that Niss was sick.

Fan, however, was too interested in making new

observations to give way weakly. For the inhabitants had surfaced with much of their household furniture: there were tables, chairs, bedsteads, wash-tubs and in fact everything made of wood.

'Look! There's a cradle – and look, look! The baby's still in it,' cried Fan as a wan green-faced Niss lifted her head. 'I'm going back to the snake pit to try and forget it,' she said. Fan went with her too.

'It's pretty grim,' she reflected. 'But it's a wonderful documentary proof of the crime that God intended when He thought up the flood.'

'Do you remember hearing Noah muttering: "safe down at the bottom of the water"? It's a good comment on that,' said Niss.

'I hope the horrible old brute is haunted by them,' said Fan.

They sat down among the snakes which seemed less lethargic and livelier since the rain had stopped. Fan caught hold of a King Cobra and began teasing it until it put up its hood. Then she stroked it and gave it a kiss and the keen little jewelled eyes looked at her without malice.

'It's all Noah's doing. Even if God planned it, Noah could have refused to commit such an appalling crime. As it is, the flood has made him. No one would have heard of him without the flood. He was a quite unremarkable old man with bad habits: by drowning everyone else he has become the most important person in existence.'

'Well, when we get off the ark we'll have nothing to do with the old beast.'

'We'll have a God of our own: a snake God,' said Fan. She held up the python by his neck and he hung down limp but full of latent strength.

'You'll live in our temple and I shall be a priestess. I'll take the swan and the raven too.'

'And the mother wolf,' said Niss.

'Good. That's settled,' said Fan. But they were restless.

Though the ark had no sails and no oars, it offered a lot of surface to the wind and as a wind got up it drifted. So the next time the sisters looked out there were no human corpses visible – only a lot of whitish lumps which had once been sheep.

That night the wind rose and choppy waves came over the waters and the ark danced sedately among them. Soon there was a great mooing and baaing and grunting, for many of the animals were in misery, the greatest sufferers seeming to be the sheep and the cattle and the camels and the pigs. The moonlight was brilliant and by its light the sisters could see that the water was full of floating trees and branches and they imagined that among them there would be the bodies of drowned woodland creatures, squirrels, martens, foxes, badgers, rabbits and deer that, like men and sheep, had been sacrificed to the indifference of God.

'Which is worse: God's wrath or His indifference?' asked Niss. Fan shrugged her shoulders.

'Both ideas are made up by people like Noah. He thinks God is nothing but an inflated version of himself.'

'But which is worse? Indifference or anger?'

'The question hasn't any meaning, Niss. Because we aren't talking about human emotions, but about the laws of nature. If God means anything, He means the laws that govern us all and which are equally true on the moon or the most distant star.'

'But if God isn't another bigger Mr Noah in the sky, how do you account for the Deluge and the ark?'

'I don't *have* to account for things,' said Fan. 'I am an ignorant girl. Probably nobody will ever know why the birds fed us in the desert and why the snakes are friendly. But I am sure it was not just because a God told them to. It was because of some big universal change, part of what produced the flood.'

'But you must have a theory,' insisted Niss.

'No. I haven't enough facts to form one. It was damned lucky for us. That's all.'

Niss was not satisfied with this. It was very reasonable but she would have liked Fan to have had a theory even if she had found it difficult to explain. And though she had lived so close to Fan – in intimate contact with her for nine months before they were born and ever since – it was strange that she could not see into Fan's mind or Fan into her's. Wondering about the mystery which makes every individual, even an identical twin, a separate person inscrutable to all

[87]

others, she fell asleep in the hay undisturbed by the bleating of sheep, groaning of camels, bellowing of cattle, or of the elephants next door rattling their chains.

It cannot be imagined that several thousands of animals could be shut up at close quarters with no exercise and insufficient food for several months together without deaths occurring amongst them. For the most part the victims were among the smaller mammals, varieties of shrewmice, hedgehogs, weasels and so forth whose disappearance went unnoticed. If a dead beast were found, Noah's sons would hastily throw the carcase overboard when their father was not looking.

But the death of the Cock Phoenix was a different matter, for the dying bird was discovered by Noah himself. The male Phoenix was the most beautiful of all the birds. His body was milky white with a faint touch of coffee, but these white feathers were shot with such hundreds of iridiscent colours that he changed colour constantly like a milky opal. Thus at one moment he flashed crimson – while in certain lights the whole bird seemed to be on fire. Noah loved it above all winged creatures.

He found it lying crumpled on the floor with its mate beating her wings despairingly trying, if the truth were known, to fan away the foetid air of prison which was poisoning her mate. Noah picked him up and came down the ladder calling to his wife. Hearing him,

Fan and Niss looked through a crack in the wall of the cat house where they chanced to be and thus saw most of what followed. Mrs Noah brought a little jug of milk. Noah set the bird on the cover of the hatchway and held open his beak while Mrs Noah poured some milk into it. But the milk spilt out again and the phoenix closed his scarlet eye and gave a terrible shiver. And as it shivered, its feathers seemed to explode into flame of every imaginable colour. A moment later it was nothing but the corpse of an ashen white bird.

When Noah saw that the male phoenix was indeed dead, he cried out in a frenzied voice to God:

'Strike me down, oh Lord, for I have betrayed Thy trust.' And for a little while he stood looking wildly up searching the different quarters of the sky expectantly. But The Lord held His hand and did not strike Noah. Then the old man wept in great sobs and tore at his beard and hair while his old wife clung to him and tried to stop him.

At last he pushed her off and said more calmly:

'No, no. I must be punished for my sin. Tell Ham to come here.' And he tore off his long robe and the shirt beneath so that his back was bare. And though he was such an old man his skin was white and without wrinkles and his bare back and shoulders were beautiful.

'Tie me,' he said when Ham came. And Ham did what he was told. 'Now scourge me,' said Noah. Ham

looked at his father oddly, but Noah said to him:
'Scourge me till I faint or I will not let thee live.'

Ham went away and came back with canes and a leather whip and he began to beat his father with the canes. But they broke, so he threw them away and scourged his father with the raw hide whip. At every stroke the blood broke through the white skin and at last the old man fell forward fainting. And he had not groaned. And while Ham was scourging his father, Shem and Japheth had to hold their mother and carry her away by force. For a week after his scourging, Noah lay in bed while Mrs Noah changed the poultices upon his back morning and night.

But on the sabbath after it Noah came out of his room pale and shaking, and he said to them assembled:

'God has forgiven me my great sin, not for my sake but for the sake of all the other birds and beasts that I serve. And because I was not content to go without punishment, He has promised me that He will work a miracle so that the Phoenix shall not perish from the earth. The hen phoenix shall live for six hundred years. And when the time comes she shall cast herself into the flames and lay an egg. And the flames that consume her shall hatch the egg and a new phoenix shall arise. But always shall she be solitary and alone and never again shall she know the joy of loving and being loved. So my sin shall be remembered forever among the Arabian sands.'

Fan woke before dawn: it was already daylight but

with the translucent unreality which pervades all
things before the sun transfigures them. There was not
a breath of that wind which had so distressed the
ruminants, not a piece of flotsam; nothing but pure
limpid water all round the ark, the sides of which were
reflected in the deep. Not an animal or a man was
stirring. She tiptoed back to the hayloft.

'Come along, Niss. Let's have a swim,' she whispered.
It was foolhardy but they had talked of it so often that
the risks had become familiar to them. Niss, still
sleepy, followed her and discarding their snakes and
their clothes, they went down a companion ladder and
slipped into the water. It was cooler than they expected but it was very soft on their skins, so soft that
it was almost oily. They swam out some way over the
smooth water being careful not to splash. The surface
broke into reluctant ripples at their touch, ripples that
spread in little undulations and rapidly disappeared.
For a time they floated on their backs looking up into
the sky. By holding a deep breath it was possible to
achieve equilibrium, with the water just below the
chin, the points of the nipples breaking surface, all else
submerged by the freshwater flood. But when they let
the air out of their lungs, the water slid over chin and
mouth and the nipples went under until a quick
breath lifted the body again.

There was nothing to see but the level expanse of
the unrippled water, with the ark in the distance,
doubled by its own reflection. As they watched, the sun

rose behind them and as it rose so the nature of the world changed. They swam quickly back being careful to make no sound. They were lucky to get back safely for before their skins were dry they heard Ham's wife scolding him and heard him a moment later clumping along the deck on his way to the hayloft. So they had to seize their shirts, jeans and snakes and dive into the hay at the back. Little bits of it clung to their goose-flesh nakedness and tickled for the rest of the morning. But Niss had left a wet footprint on the deck and as he went to the stable Shem noticed it. He looked at it sleepily, without suspicion and went on. But the memory remained in his mind and an hour later he went back to look. The sun had fallen on it and it had dried leaving no trace.

'Could be that boy Gomer,' he reflected.

Gomer brought them food to the hayloft and all three of them nestled down in the big hole in which they spent much of their time. Gomer sat a little apart watching the hungry girls who ate unself-consciously, cramming their mouths full of lentils, spitting out olive stones, cracking nuts with their teeth. The mother wolf had long since gone dry so they pleaded to Gomer to bring them a little milk which he found difficult: first to steal it and then to climb high up through the slippery hay without spilling it from the little jug. When he had brought it the sisters always gave their snakes the first drink and Gomer watched with fascinated horror as Niss tipped the jug a little sideways so that the asp could drink without putting its head down into the jug, for the serpent was wary and liked to look about him as he drank. When the asp had taken its fill, Niss passed the jug to Fan so that her Russell's viper could drink in the same dainty way. Gomer watching, could see the slender neck swell and contract three or four times as the mouthfuls of milk went down its throat. When it had finished, Fan put the jug to her own lips and swallowed what was left leaving none for Niss.

' Pooh, you don't want a serpent's leavings,' she said when her sister protested and Niss, looking at her steadily said: 'Liar, pig, hog.' Fan did not mind these epithets but she looked at her sister in sudden rage when she was called a monkey.

In the very top of the hayloft was a shelf and exploring there, Niss found three big earthenware pipes, each about a foot in diameter and about a yard long. The ends were closed with clay except for a narrow slot with a little shelf below it. These were colonies of bees, for in those days and, for long afterwards in those parts, bees were kept in clay pipes. During the rains the bees had been quiet enough, but as the warmer days came on, they began stirring, though there was no way of their getting out into the sunlight and there were no flowers from which they could gather honey if they did. These bees did not seem to have been told that they had to be peaceable aboard the ark and to be gentle to mankind: Niss and

Fan were each stung and so, to their delight, was Ham when he swished a forkful of hay past their dwellings.

One morning another gale sprang up and once again the ark resounded with cries of distress as it rolled heavily in the trough of a long wave. A sudden violent gust blew the door of the monkey house open and before Mrs Japheth could run to shut it, a score of apes and baboons had bounded out and rushed about the ark insane with delight. Some were chased and captured and put back. The others took refuge in the ridge of the roof where they ran about chattering like sailors. But they did not relish the cold wind and half an hour later they had all gone back into the monkey house of their own accord. Fan and Niss did not feel alarmed as they had their snakes handy. So, ignoring the monkeys they cowered in a hidden spot in the lee of the stables where they could see over the waters and where no one ever came except to fetch the holystones to scrub down the deck.

They sat there out of the wind looking at the waves. Suddenly they caught sight of something black appear and disappear among the waves.

'It was alive,' said Fan.

'Too big for a man,' said Niss.

'Miles too big.'

A few moments later the black object leaped from the crest of a wave and returned almost instantly. Then another black thing some way behind the first, leaped out, bent over and disappeared and another close to that one. Altogether they counted four of the creatures. They were dolphins, or porpoises, creatures which had been able to save themselves during the flood without Noah's help. The porpoises turned out not to be the only creatures of the kind. One morning the air was full of seagulls. Some of the birds were circling about the ark, some perched on the roof. They had pale grey plumage and yellow feet and legs and yellow ceres at the base of their bills. And they stared stonily at everything. Noah heard their screaming and came out of his pilot house and the sight of the birds infuriated him. He waved his hands at them and cursed them, but as they did not pay him any attention he brought out an ancient crossbow and tried to shoot one of them. But his old hands trembled with feeble rage and when he shot, the quarrel went a foot wide and was lost in the waters.

After staying with the ark for the greater part of the day, the seagulls suddenly disappeared one by one and were not seen again.

Then, one morning two hours before dawn when the sisters went for an early morning swim, a sleek round head suddenly came up out of the water close beside them and stared at them with big, lustrous dark eyes. For the first moment Niss thought it was a big dog, but then she saw that it was a seal. It kept disappearing in the water and then putting its head out again. The sisters were so accustomed to treating all the most dangerous and fierce animals as friends, that each time it came up they swam towards it and put out their hands to touch it. Fan even spoke to it, calling: 'Good dog. Good dog, come here.'

But it was shy and each time it dived away, only to come up a moment or two later out of reach.

It occurred to Fan that in the ark all the animals were under a special commandment – or subject to an instinct – or perhaps somehow hypnotised – to be gentle with man and with each other for their mutual good. But this seal was not of their number and was still truly a wild creature, untouched by grace and neglected by God and Noah. Yet though it would not let them touch it, the seal was not unfriendly and seemed to play with them, though its staring eyes made it seem solemn in its play. After they had regained the ark and dressed, they heard Shem come on deck, and he must have seen the creature for he called out to Ham: 'If I had the old man's crossbow, I would shoot the thing. I expect the meat is good enough eating.'

'I'll have a go with my sling,' said Ham. They could not watch, for the seal was on the other side of the ark but they heard a splash and a curse from Ham which told them that he had missed the stranger. After that the seal did not come back to experiment further in making acquaintance with mankind. And then one evening in the distance they saw a jet of water being thrown into the air, but they could not think of an explanation for they knew nothing of whales.

The months of captivity were slipping by and though there was no indication by which they could know it, the waters were subsiding. And the hay in the loft was being used up fast so that it was nine-tenths empty. Then one day Ham found their hiding place. They were away that afternoon asleep with their old friends the lions whom they only visited after Japheth had given their cage an airing and had swept away the soiled straw and gnawed bones. Niss was lying with her head between the lioness's paws and Fan with her's supported by the tiger's belly, when they heard a shouting and Shem and Japheth running. Some minutes later the brothers came along the outside deck talking excitedly.

'Eggshells everywhere. They must have lived on eggs,' said Ham.

'They must have swum to the ark and have been living here for months,' said Japheth.

'Noah will have something to say to God about this,' said Shem. Then the voices were no longer distinguishable. After that the sisters lived almost entirely in the snake pit, only coming out at dead of night to meet Gomer in the pony's stable with food. The boy had been crossquestioned by Noah, been threatened with a beating by Japheth and had his arm twisted by Ham, but he had steadily denied any knowledge of stow-aways on board.

After a week in the snake pit, the sisters felt that they could not endure life any longer without a swim

[97]

and an hour before Gomer was to bring food to the aviary (where it occurred to them that the birds could be relied on to pick up all the crumbs they might drop), they slipped gently overboard.

It was a windless night; the half moon was low, the water warm after a day of hot spring sunshine. They swam a long way from the ark in silence so that it would be safe to talk in freedom. In the snake pit they dared only converse in sibilant whispers, for fear of being overheard by Mrs Noah who had a window box with flowers a few yards away and was always fussing over them and calling to Noah to come and look at a newly opened tulip or geranium.

The old man would stand, apparently deaf as a post, but when she had bustled in to the living-room, he would sometimes walk up to the window box, look at the flower in question and spit over the side. Niss, listening intently, once heard him grunt and murmur: ' Beats me why the old 'ooman's that stuck on flaars,' and spit again.

They talked quietly. Fan believed their imprisonment would not last more than a few weeks. The hay was nearly all gone and Noah seemed to be brisking up. Then they swam slowly back. They were tired out as they climbed up the companion ladder and stood on the deck. It was a strain being hidden for so long and they were feeling it. The next moment a cord net had fallen over them and there was a shout of excitement from Ham. They were knocked down, rolled up in the net and trapped. It was dark under the bulwark where they lay. A hand gripped Niss by the arm, she twisted forward, caught one of the fingers with her teeth through the net and bit with all her might. Shem screamed, tore his hand away and kicked at the netting.

'Bring a light,' commanded Japheth.

'Let me club 'im,' said Ham eagerly.

'Put that club down, Ham,' said Japheth. Shem came back with a lantern still cursing about his bitten finger.

'Let's see what we've got,' said Japheth.

'Club 'im first and look later,' said Ham.

Shem shone the lamp on the heap under the net.

'Hey. There's two on 'em,' said Ham.

'My! We've caught us a couple of girls,' said Shem. The three men stared in silence at the two naked girls in the net.

'They might show some sport,' said Ham at last and Shem laughed unpleasantly.

'What do you think they are?' asked Japheth. Then, taking the lantern from Shem, he shone it on the girls' faces.

'I've seen them before,' he said. 'Why, it is those twins that used to hang about when we were fitting the ark out.'

'No reason we shouldn't have our fun with them before we chuck 'em back,' said Ham. But his proposal was cut short by the voice of Mrs Ham.

'Whatever are you men doing there, so early?' she

[99]

asked, coming forward to look. She was followed by Mrs Shem.

When the women realised that the net contained two girls stark naked, they rounded furiously on their husbands.

' A pretty piece of work, you filthy bare-faced devil! ' cried Mrs Ham.

' Caught you in the act,' chimed in Mrs Shem.

' Had two girls hidden on board all these months! '

' Carrying on under our noses! '

' Looks as though now we are getting near land they have got frightened and planning to drown 'em.'

' I'd divorce you if there were only another man in the world to be had, which there ain't,' said Mrs Ham. ' So don't you think you can get away from me.'

' I'll go straight to Noah. He'll have these little tarts whipped and then drowned,' said Mrs Shem.

' We have only just caught them. They came here swimming and climbed up the ladder on to the deck,' said Japheth.

' That's a likely tale! ' exclaimed Mrs Ham. ' You ought to be ashamed, Japheth. You're supposed to be better than your brothers.'

' You men would stick together,' said Mrs Shem.

' Swimming for nearly four months! That's a tall story. You tell Noah that and see what he says to it.'

' Well, cover up their nakedness, they aren't fit to show to Noah like that,' said a calm voice. Mrs Japheth had joined the group but had said nothing till then.

The sun had risen. Now she went back into the ark and returned with two torn shirts of her husband's and two skirts of her own. The net was lifted and Fan and Niss allowed to put on the clothes, which they did reluctantly. They had not spoken a word the whole time.

'Go and fetch father,' Japheth said to his wife. When at length Noah arrived the shouts and abuse of Mrs Ham and the tears of Mrs Shem, subsided into mutterings and whimpers.

'Just give the word and I'll club 'em on the head and sling 'em overboard. The sooner they go the better. These wives of ours are crazy. And we never knew what we had in the net till Shem fetched a lantern.'

Noah said nothing. His eyes were heavy with sleep and his beard tousled and untidy. He looked at the sisters with glazed, unseeing eyes.

'Tie 'em up in that loose box. I'll settle 'em myself some time.' The old man turned on his heel and went back to bed.

The sisters were tied up in a disused pigstye. Though the filth had been shovelled overboard and the floor scrubbed, the place still smelt strongly of hog. Fan and Niss were connoisseurs in the effluvia of the animal kingdom and they rated pig among the worst. They were bruised, Fan had been kicked in the side by Ham – they were dirty and livid with rage. Nevertheless they soon fell asleep and it was with astonishment that when they woke up they saw it was already afternoon.

The sun beat in, striping the floor through narrow louvres in the roof overhead. Fan shifted to one side and the rope which had been holding her parted. She looked at it in astonishment. While she had been asleep some little friend, rat or mouse perhaps, had crept in and gnawed the rope asunder.

'I'm free,' she whispered to Niss. 'I can untie you.'

But after she had disentangled her hands and feet and looked at the door of the pigstye, she found it was securely bolted and barred from the outside. They could not hope to escape, nor could they hide on the ark when their presence was known. They would be hunted down and surrounded.

'We had better keep the ropes round our wrists and ankles so that when Noah comes he will think that we are still tied up,' said Niss.

Fan nodded. They arranged the ropes so that they could throw them off quickly. While they were doing this there was a warning hiss and they looked up to see their familiar snakes slipping under the badly fitting door and slowly gliding up to them. They threw off the ropes, took their protectors in their hands, held them to their mouths, kissed them and were kissed in return by the little vivid flickering forked tongues. Niss even opened her mouth and popped her asp's head in and touched him with her tongue and then laughed, kissed him again, hid the faithful serpent in the bosom of her old shirt and rearranged the ropes about her wrists.

From the depths of despair and self-contempt the prisoners became jubilant and began to long for the interview with Noah in which they would unexpectedly have the advantage on their side.

Hours went by. The bars of sunlight left the floor and crept up the wall of the pigstye. At last they heard a sharp tapping footstep, the door was unlocked and Mrs Noah stood in the doorway.

'Had a good sleep, dearies?' she asked. They stared at her in her stiff red skirt, with a blue apron over it and her doll's face with apple cheeks and black hair plastered to her skull.

'He's just coming, dearies, don't be frightened. There's no real harm in him. Just you do what he wants . . .' She paused and then went on: 'It's nothing really, you know . . . I don't think he'll drown you,' she added brightly.

The two girls looked at her without speaking. Mrs Noah produced a little jug which she had been holding beneath her apron. 'Here's a drop of something that will do you good. Only don't tell him I gave it you,' she said hurriedly and ashamed.

The twins exchanged a warning look. After their experience when Ephraim drugged them and abandoned them in the desert they were taking no risks on drinking strange mixtures.

'Just water, please,' said Fan.

'A drop of wine would do you a world of good. And make you fall in with what Noah wants. You might enjoy it too. You know, it might amuse you to see what a man's like. Of course he's old. But he's a fine man still.'

The sisters said nothing and Mrs Noah went out and came back with a pitcher of water. They drank deeply.

'Ah, I can hear him moving. It won't do for him to find me here. Remember, don't be frightened.' And Mrs Noah took the pitcher and hurried away.

The old man came stumbling down the passage, he breathed heavily and opened the door. For some time he stood there leaning uncertainly and staring at them with bright blue eyes in his scarlet face. He had combed his long beard and occasionally he licked the red full lips that were almost concealed by it.

'Now what may you be?' he soliloquised. 'Water witches sent to tempt me by Satan, or a consolation and reward for my good work, sent by The Lord? He knows I need you badly enough. Shut up here for nearly five months with my family and a lot of stinking animals. I used to like animals. I could have stood it for a month – but I've been near five months and all the time my life is slipping away. The lust of the flesh. It don't matter when you are a young man. You know you'll have all you want in time. You can afford to pick and choose. But when you are getting on into your seventh century it's dreadful to feel you are losing your last chance . . . God will have understood that and sent you as a reward . . .' he muttered. He tottered up to Niss and put out his withered claw to lift her smock. But as he did so, she slipped her wrists free of the ropes and held out the asp from her bosom.

Fan scrambled to her feet and in a moment they had crowded the old man into a corner of the pigstye.

Noah was unabashed and his attention was more for the serpents than for the girls brandishing them.

'You dare threaten me!' he exclaimed, pointing his finger at the Russell's viper. 'And you would have been drowned and all your accursed seed lost for ever, but for the loving kindness I have shown you.'

The viper opened its mouth widely to exhibit its fangs, yawned and then hissed in answer.

'There's gratitude! That is the reward I am given. You ought to be ashamed . . .'

Fan took the old man by the shoulders, pulled him forward, and tripped him so that he fell on to the floor. He sat up quickly. 'May you be barren, you devil's spawn,' he cursed.

Then he continued his soliloquy with increasing dignity. 'If I had been what you think, just a lecher, I would have built the ark for my pleasure. I would have filled it with musicians playing on shawms and dulcimers and with dancing girls in silken raiment and it would have been scented with nard and ambergris and sweet odours. And I should have bathed in rose water and ass's milk. I should have chosen a thousand concubines from the most lovely girls of all the races in the world, and I should have peopled the earth anew from my own loins. But because I was a man who listened to God's voice and thought nothing of my own pleasure, I filled the ark with fierce beasts with tusks and claws, covered in bristles and rough hair, all foully stinking after their kind, polecats and such, all filling the ark with their discordant cries and I have lived with my old woman and my three dull, good-for-nothing sons and their hateful wives . . . I have foresworn pleasure and all for the sake of others and for the generations of man and beast to come. And now this is my reward.' Noah looked upwards and it was evident that he was addressing not the sisters or the snakes, but God.

'Yes. This is the reward You give Your faithful servant. Who else would have listened to You? Who else would have built You an ark? Where could You have found another damned fool like me? Answer me that. Nowhere. And now that the waters are sinking You play this damned trick on me. And when the land is dry You will cast Your servant aside because his work is done. Well and truly done. You are a jealous God.'

'Let's go,' whispered Niss. For the first time she felt sorry for Noah and was afraid that if she stayed pity might grow into liking. Fan had no such tenderness and walked out first. Niss turned on the threshold. 'Good-bye, old man,' she said. They ran undetected to the great aviary in the roof. Noah did not appear to notice their departure, but his next words showed that he had.

'I'm as fine a man as ever I was and those little sluts run off. And a few months ago I could have had the pick of all the women in the world. I ought to have filled the ark with them. I'm still what any sensible woman wants. I'm not old . . .'

'Of course you are not,' said Mrs Noah, who had come back when she saw the sisters slip away. 'You're as young as the day I married you.'

'What, you here? You wooden image,' said Noah crossly. And then he suddenly burst out: 'I can't bear it. I can't bear it. I love life and all living things. I saved them all from God's wrath and because I'm old . . .' He broke into violent sobs.

'There, there, have a drink and maybe you'll forget it,' said Mrs Noah and handed him a jug. Noah drank. After a little he dried his tears. 'I'll drown that pair if ever I get my hands on them,' he said reflectively.

'Don't talk of drowning. There have been enough people drowned already to my way of thinking,' said Mrs Noah severely. But the outbursts of emotion had been too much and in a few minutes her husband was asleep.

Next morning, for the first time the sisters went openly about the ark – but with their snakes either in their hands or about their necks. If Ham chanced to see them, he shouted abuse at them, but Fan and Niss stood their ground and seeing the snakes, their enemy cursed them and went stumbling on his way. Shem, on seeing them threw up his arms, made a face and spat; Noah turned his back, or pretended not to see them and to their sorrow Japheth followed his father's example. The three younger women pointed at them and jabbered to each other; only old Mrs Noah smiled and showed them kindness. The first time she caught sight of them she called out and when they went up to her she gave them each a bowl of soup and a crust of bread to dip in it and told them that if they came back later she would have something more for them.

They waited for Gomer at their usual dinner hour but he did not come. After waiting two hours they went in search of him but could find him nowhere. Then it occurred to Niss that he might have been punished on their account and they went to the pig-stye where they had been kept prisoners. There the boy was, as they could tell by an occasional sob and muffled howl of rage. They called to him and he stopped blubbering when he heard their voices and only whispered: 'Don't make any noise. I shall get another beating if they hear me speak to you.'

Later he explained that Noah had ordered that he should be given a beating and that his father had left it to Shem, who had thrashed him until the blood came, had ordered him never to speak to either of the twins on pain of being flogged to death because they were demons – the progeny of an angel and a woman who was more beautiful than she should be. It was,

Noah said, to rid the earth of such monstrous creatures that God had ordained the deluge.

As Gomer thought they were the most lovely beings that he had ever seen, and as it was obvious that they had only escaped drowning by a subterfuge, he did not question what Shem told him. Indeed, nothing seemed more probable. However, Gomer was a strong-minded lad and was ready to side with the daughters of an angel against his family. So after Fan and Niss had broken open the door of the pigstye and untied him, he went with them willingly enough, after first pulling up his shirt and pulling down his trousers to show them what he had suffered on their account.

'You must live with us all the time now,' said Niss.

Gomer gulped down his emotion. 'How are you going to live unless I get you food?' he asked.

'Your granny will give us enough to get along with and it won't be long before we get out of this stinking ark,' said Fan.

'Then all three of us will go away together,' said Niss.

'My God, I hate all my family. I don't know what I should do if I hadn't got you,' he said.

The waters were subsiding fast and all on board the ark first realised it when they grounded for a few moments one evening on the summit of Mount Ararat, though of course they had not any idea what the bottom was dragging on. For a few moments the ark stuck: there was a high wind and the waves broke violently on one side and the whole ark took a list which became greater and greater. And then it slipped off into deep water. For three days they watched the mountain tops rise out of the water beside them: the sharp cone of Little Ararat appeared and was recognised by Noah. And beside them was the wall of the great mountain.

One morning when the sisters and Gomer were in the aviary, Noah marched in and, paying them no attention, seized one of the ravens, opened the window and dropped the bird out. It flew away and was not seen again.

A week later Noah burst in again, scowled at them saying: 'Still here?' and turned to take one of the doves off its perch. He stroked it gently and released it out of the window. The sisters were not surprised to see it fluttering round the ark all day: it was the mating season and the dove had been billing and cooing and strutting and ruffling up his feathers in front of his mate for days past. In the evening Noah opened the window and the dove flew in looking all the better for stretching his wings. A week later Noah put the same dove out again and this time it returned with a twig of olive in his beak: not very surprising since his mate had started to build a nest on one of the cross beams and the olive twig was for that. A week later, when the hen was sitting, Noah put the dove out for a third time and he did not return.

Part Three

THE sisters and Gomer left the ark before the dove. To do so was not easy as the lowest deck was a full twenty feet above the ground, and as the ark was resting in a hollow it was still surrounded by a huge pool of water. Gomer found a rope which he passed round the bottom of the companion ladder. Niss swarmed down it first, Fan followed. They found themselves waist deep in water but the bottom was firm. Gomer lowered three bundles with the possessions they had been collecting in order to start life in the new postdiluvian world. They had all been stolen – but they had to have them: a wooden fire-drill with a box of tinder, a knife each, needles and thread, a cooking pot and frying pan, a skin of water, a blanket each, fish hooks and a fishing line which Gomer had woven from hairs from the tail of the white Arab stallion. Lastly came Gomer himself. He pulled the rope after him.

When the ark had slid off the crest of Ararat, it had come to rest on a shoulder of the mountain, just above the birch forest which grew on the lower slopes.

It was early summer, but owing to the flood the

seasons were all mixed up. Very few of the drowned trees and plants had recovered sufficiently to put out leaves or flowers: the majority were dead and everywhere their branches were draped with curtains of flotsam left hanging to dry by the retreating waters. Nevertheless, seeds buried in the earth before the flood had germinated and many were already pushing their way into the sunlight. Gomer and the sisters had come out too soon. But they could not go back, confess to their thefts and plead for admission.

'We are the only people walking about the earth,' said Fan.

Their way through the forest, but their passage was everywhere barred by a tangle of uprooted saplings and branches which had fallen upon and broken down the tops of the larger trees. The forest was impassable and they soon realised that if they ventured far into it they might be lost for ever. They wandered along the edge until they came to where a stream cut its way down the mountain. The way was steep and rocky, but Gomer pointed out that if they followed the stream they could not get lost and wander in circles. They fastened the rope to their waists so that there was no fear of losing each other and that if the leader fell the other two could hold her from falling far. Then, taking turns to lead, they scrambled first to one side, then to the other of the bed of the stream, climbing over or under the uprooted trees that barred the way, but always getting lower down.

At last the leader of the three, who at that moment was Niss, came to a sort of tunnel and wading in the stream, under the barricade of uprooted trees and boulders wedged by them in the air, crawled out on to a rocky hillside above a small lake, the water of which reflected the blue sky.

They were exhausted, scratched from thorns, bruised by tumbles on the rocks and were overjoyed to find a place where they could camp and rest.

Time was needed before the world could recover and as the three sat round their fire and talked, they felt, in spite of their physical exhaustion, for the first time a great fear and a loneliness which was not less because there were three of them. What are three people on an empty, lifeless planet which has been ruined and which will need time before it becomes fit to live in? There was madness in the smashed-up, broken, tangled forest, a madness which they had not foreseen when they were imprisoned in the little world of the ark. Noah was wise to be waiting for the healing touch of time before daring to venture out or to liberate the hordes of starving animals. They would have done better to have been patient – but for them there could be no going back. Indeed, as Fan lay awake listening to her companions sleeping, she felt that she would rather face the chaos all about her than return to the foetid prison higher up on the shoulder of the mountain. She slept and the moon rose, but she woke some hours later and a feverish excitement came over her. She stood up silently, being careful not to wake the others and walked down to the edge of the lake. The full moon riding remote in the sky and its reflection in the unrippled water held the madness of loneliness: she was aware of infinite space, of the emptiness of an unchanging universe, and she gazed frozen.

Suddenly, not twenty yards away from where she stood on the shore, a big trout leapt from the water and fell back with a splash. Ripples spread over the lake breaking the reflection of the moon into a lane of silver light.

Fan's heart leapt with pleasure; the loneliness of the devastated earth was gone; there were fish.

That trout rising for a fly altered the world for all three of them. For next morning, when Fan told of her discovery, Gomer went quickly to the edge of the forest and cut himself a wand of hazel to the end of which he tied the horsehair line which tapered down to three long hairs. The only earthworms left on the whole globe were a pair which had by chance got into Mrs Noah's window-box. Gomer could not have known this, but he had whiled away some hours in the ark in making fish hooks out of porcupine quill tips, which he had dressed with a parrot's red tail feather.

Niss and Fan collected wood for a fire while Gomer cast his lure over the lake. A trout took it under water and the first that Gomer knew was the pull of the line. Then the trout was rushing about bending his hazel this way and that, fighting hard while he tried to lead it in a circle. He kept his line tight but made no attempt to pull the fish ashore until he saw it turn on its side. Only then did Gomer draw it to the edge of the lake and, bending down, he scraped the fish out of the water with his free hand, throwing it inland. The hook came out and the trout was bending double and leaping over the turf back towards the water.

Ten minutes later the fish was frying in the pan and filling the air with a delicious smell that made their mouths water.

The three weeks which the three spent camping beside the lake were happy although most of their time was spent in hunting for food. And the necessity for that kept them from quarrelling. They were busy. Gomer rose a couple of hours before dawn and began fishing while it was still almost dark and went on until the heat of the risen sun put the fish down. He slept in the middle of the day and began fishing again with the evening rise. One morning when the white vapour still hung over the lake, Gomer was sitting on a rock almost half asleep, waiting for the first breeze to blow the mist away when he saw big ripples spreading and a small dark head swimming towards him. It was an otter. Noah had taken a pair of otters into the ark and Gomer knew them well. But this beast was one of the illegitimate animals which had refused drowning in the Deluge. No doubt he had been able to rest and sleep and eat the fish he caught, on the trunk of a floating tree. During the months of flood the fish had grown fat on the abundance of good food which it had brought them: all the earthworms, all the wasps' nests and anthills in the world, not to speak of the carcasses of all the quadrupeds, men and birds. And filled with food and delivered from most of their enemies the fish had multiplied enormously without waiting for specific instructions as to spawning from God. After that first morning, all three of them often saw the otter and his mate playing together in the lake in the evening. And they rejoiced to see another warm-blooded creature and sometimes Fan whistled to them in the hopes that they would come ashore and make friends. But they paid no attention to her.

Like the otters the three truants lived on fish, though they gathered sprouting seeds for salads, rejecting those which tasted nauseous and boiling young nettles and sowthistles.

Then for two days Gomer was unlucky in his fishing and they had nothing but ground-up bark and grass. On the third night all three lay awake unable to sleep for hunger and they rose gloomily when it was light. Gomer had not caught a fish or he would have brought it back at once. But going to look for him Niss found the knoll above the lake white with button mushrooms! So they managed to keep alive, and that evening Gomer, who had again had a blank day, robbed the otter of a big sturgeon. But they longed for bread, for honey and for milk.

One day as they rested in the middle of the day,

they heard a rush of wings and, looking up, saw birds of every kind about them. In the sky the wings of golden plover scissored against the blue, from the woods a couple of golden pheasants and a pair of peafowl burst like rockets; little birds; finches and warblers were flitting from tree to rock and rock to tree all about them. A pair of swans circled and dropped and alighted with dragging feet in the lake and rode there in beauty.

'Noah must have let all the birds out,' said Fan.

'He'll be letting all the animals loose next,' said Gomer.

'I shall go back to see that. I would not miss it for the world,' said Niss.

'We must all go,' said Fan.

'So long as he doesn't see us,' said Gomer, worried.

'What does it matter? He'll have his hands too full to bother about us,' said Fan.

Next morning they set off to climb the bed of the stream which they had descended with so much difficulty in order to get back to the shoulder of the mountain on which the ark rested. They found that climbing up was easy compared with climbing down. Moreover they knew the way. Even so they were late for the beginning of the liberation of the animals for a whole army of mice, rats and squirrels rushed past them into the birch forest.

Noah had released the smallest and most defenceless animals first so as to give them a good start ahead of their natural enemies, the predators. After the small animals he planned to release the vegetarians and only when they had disappeared would he liberate the weasels, martens, stoats, polecats, ferrets and foxes. Then he planned to let out wolves, wild cats, lynxes, leopards, tigers and lions, and then, last of all the reptiles and serpents.

All this took time. On their arrival they saw that they had forgotten the enormous size of the ark. Its wooden walls rose up like those of a citadel. The three decks rose one above the other and through the portholes and over the rails were the heads of hundreds of watching animals, many of them friends of Fan and Niss. Seeing them, they bellowed, roared, barked, whinnied, so that the arrival of the sisters and Gomer gave rise to pandemonium. Fan called out and waved to the lioness and the she-wolf, but Gomer caught hold of her and pulled her behind a bush.

' You're crazy. We're done for if any of them spot us,' he whispered. They lay and looked at the huge ark with the roof rising forty feet above the level of the ground. Then, seeing that none of the humans had noticed them, Gomer and the two girls climbed up a side of the mountain behind the ark to a flat place where they could be hidden and out of the way, where they lay on their bellies with their faces between their palms and their elbows propping them up. From there they could look down on the gangway which Noah and his sons had lowered in the middle of the lower deck.

Just after they took up their position, out came the pigs, squealing and rushing from side to side. But faced with Ham on one side and Japheth on the other, armed with pitchforks, they dashed into the forest. Then came a delay as Noah had changed his plans. After ten minutes a pair of rhinoceroses were prodded down the gangway and they too vanished into the forest with a great crackling of twigs. When all the rhinoceroses had been got rid of the hippopotamuses came sliding down the gangway which bent under their weight. And they also ventured in the forest and there was a renewed crackling of branches. When they had gone from hearing, the elephants came one after the other, treading warily, waving their trunks and looking about them with crafty little eyes. Realising that they were free the bull elephants trumpeted and they all disappeared into the birch forest.

They made less noise in breaking down the forest than any of the beasts which had gone before them. The reason for sending the largest and most powerful of the animals out into the forest out of their turn, was because Noah thought that they would be strong enough to bulldoze a road through the tangle of fallen trees in which many of the more delicate creatures might otherwise have been trapped. The old man was, as usual, right, and where Gomer and the twins had taken the best part of a day to climb down the stream to reach the lake, the elephants and hippos made a road which enabled the deer and cattle to reach it in an hour.

There was a long wait after the elephants had gone: then a pair of tiny mouse-deer scampered off heading a procession of gazelles, antelopes, roe-deer and deer of all varieties, ibex, goats, sheep, wild cattle, yaks, buffaloes, bison. Only after the last of the ruminants had been liberated and the gangplank of the ark drawn up and barricaded did the three watchers discover that they were dying of hunger and thirst and that their limbs were cramped and shot through with pins and needles so that they could scarcely stagger to their feet. The wind blew cold off Ararat, they shivered, they trembled with fatigue, were faint with hunger, had to spend the night miserably, yet they were filled with the wonder and glory of what they had seen. Noah, whatever his faults, however much he had been responsible for the destruction of the world, or had condoned it in the first place, had saved the animals, had given each kind its chance of survival, impartially, to the best of his ability. And they were witnessing his triumph.

Next morning they were almost light-headed with hunger and the misery of numb limbs and fingers, when the sun rose and slowly restored them to life. And immediately Noah began to let out the predators: weasels, stoats, polecats, ferrets, martens, badgers, wild cats, genets, mink, foxes, wolves, jackals, leopards, panthers, pumas, lions and tigers. Then came the monkeys. They waited, jabbering, pointing at Noah and his sons, chasing each other with lewd intent. They formed a hostile crowd and though Noah shouted at them and Ham waved a stick, they would not disperse.

Suddenly Noah released the snakes. As the first serpent glided down the gangway, the mob of monkeys broke up in a *sauve qui peut*, each running for dear life to the edge of the forest and swinging into the bushes and then into the treetops. In three minutes they were all gone and there was no sign of their passage but the top of a birch shaking violently as the last monkey sprang from it deeper into the forest.

'Our snakes,' murmured Niss and Fan together. It was difficult to see in that rippling, scaly mass, the friends who had stood by them in their direst peril. Now they were no longer so badly needed perhaps they would not be so devoted. One day they would meet a serpent face to face and cautiously find out if the old friendship was remembered.

'I want to find my snake again,' murmured Fan.

Last of all the wild creatures were again the tortoises and, before they had put many yards between themselves and the end of the gangway, Noah's sons came out leading a bullock, a ram, and a billy goat. They built an altar of loose rocks piled on top of each other, and on it lit a fire of dead rhododendron branches and birch twigs and logs. Then while Ham held its halter,

Shem cut the tendons of the bullock's hindlegs, hamstringing it with two quick blows of the axe, and Noah thrust his long knife into its throat, cutting the artery. In a little while the beast was dead and while Japheth was skinning it, the others held the ram and the billy goat and Noah killed them with his knife. The bullock was split in two down the backbone and half was carried back into the ark. The entrails and the other side of beef were heaped onto the fire. Then two smaller fires were built and half the ram and half the goat carried back for Noah's family and the rest heaped up to roast upon the fires.

Soon the smell of roasting meat rose up to the rock where Gomer and the sisters lay and they grew faint with longing. For hours they had been in torment while the shadows lengthened and the sun sank, and the fires flickered in the darkness. But at last the fires were low and Noah and his sons had gone back into the silent, empty ark and the three began to climb stiffly down in the darkness. A pebble slipped under Niss's feet and she would have fallen if Gomer had not caught her and then helped her, climbing down first and putting her toes in holes in the rock which she could not have seen in daylight, let alone at night. When she was safely down he went back and brought Fan down also.

Weak and faint, trembling with fatigue and eagerness, they pulled a great leg of the roasted ox off the altar and when Gomer had cut away the charred outside, he cut each of them a hot bloody steak. As they sucked up the gravy and cut tough lumps off to chew, life came back to them. They were drunk with food. After the first steak each of them cut another and when that was gone a third. Then, when they could eat no more the sisters yawned and would have fallen asleep if it had not been for Gomer.

'Rouse yourselves; we must keep out of Noah's clutches. He would have dearly liked to sacrifice us to The Lord and have saved the ox and ram and billy goat for himself. Come on.' And seizing Niss he dragged her to her feet and pushed her towards the forest. Then he went back for Fan, and by pushing and pulling them alternately he got them hidden among the branches of a fallen tree. Leaving them there asleep he went back to purloin a leg of roast mutton to serve as provision for the next day.

In the morning they were awakened by the voices of Ham and his wife quarrelling with each other by the altars, pulling the burnt offerings out of the embers.

'Silly old soak, leaving all that good meat for the wolves and jackals. Gosh, they have made off with a leg of mutton. It would have done nicely for my dinner. Silly old soak.'

'You be careful how you talk about Father. You never think of me. If you get yourself in trouble who is going to help me? You never think about anyone except yourself,' said his wife.

They went off with Ham growling and Mrs Ham

whining, but before Gomer and the sisters could escape, Shem and his wife came out into the forest collecting firewood. Shem was complaining of all the work which was put on him in his reedy voice and his wife was the plump echo of his woes. But before they went in Shem told his wife:

'He said last night that God was going to promise him anything he wanted. I guess he believes in striking while the iron's hot, for if he doesn't get what he wants out of God now, he'll never get it. And I fancy that thanks to the way he's pulled off this job, he's The Lord's blue-eyed boy. So we must keep a respectful tongue in our heads.'

'Just so,' said Mrs Shem. 'We know which side our bread's buttered which is more than that oaf Ham and his wife do. Did you notice that she had a leg of goat which she hid under her apron? Just think of stealing the burnt offering! Where should we be if it hadn't been for The Lord – and for Father too of course.'

They went back with their loads of firewood and Gomer and the two girls were able to steal away down the path which the elephants had made through the forest just as they heard Noah ringing the bell for prayers.

When they came out of the elephant trail and looked down at the lake they saw that it was full of animals. Four elephants were standing up to their arm-pits in the water and pouring it over their backs with

[126]

their trunks and flapping their ears. Gomer and the sisters stood rooted: then they noticed half a dozen antelopes drinking and a water buffalo wallowing. Shortly afterwards a hippopotamus surfaced and swam slowly across the lake to the other side where his mate joined him later. It was clear that Gomer could not go fishing that evening. So he brought out the leg of mutton. While they were eating a stick came flying at them from the top of a neighbouring tree. There were the monkeys to reckon with! Fan and Niss slung several stones into the forest, but as they could not tell which tree the stick had been thrown from, there was no hope of hitting their assailant.

They moved out of the forest far enough to be out of range of monkey throwers, but close enough to take shelter if the elephants should resent their being in the neighbourhood. Then they lit a fire, and sat watching and dozing alternately. At last Fan got up and strolled down to where they had hidden their belongings before going back to the ark. She took the bucket and walked down to the lake and filled it. The bull Indian elephant was standing in the water not more than thirty yards away. He watched her out of his piggy eyes, put his great ears forward as though he were angry and took a step towards her. But he did not charge. Fan turned her back on him and walked back to the others with the bucket of water, whistling to keep up her courage. Already their relations with the animals were very different from what they had been.

All three of them were tired out and they slept before sunset and did not wake next day until it was afternoon. The lake was deserted with no sign of any animals. The sun was shining. But just then down came a sharp shower of rain sparkling in the sunshine and over the far end of the lake the first rainbow.

They stared at it astonished and then, one by one, they went wild with delight.

'That's a sign,' said Gomer.

'What of?' asked Fan, trying to keep her head.

'That the bloody old world is different now,' said Niss.

The shower stopped, the rainbow hung for a minute or two in the sky and then faded away so slowly that they kept imagining that it was still there after it had gone.

'Go and catch us a fish,' suggested Niss.

'No fishing. We've got to get moving quickly. At any moment all the Noahs will be coming down here,' said Gomer sharply.

'Why do you think that?' asked Fan. 'You don't think that they'll live in the ark for ever, do you? Noah will want to get a long way south and out of the mountains before winter sets in. Otherwise they'll get snowed up.'

Niss nodded agreement.

'How do you know we are north of where we started from?' asked Fan.

'There was a south-west wind almost all the months

that we were in the ark. And I heard Mrs Noah saying that Noah had recognised the peak of Little Ararat. Come on. Pack up and we'll get moving.'

'I expect you are right,' said Fan reluctantly. She did not care for Gomer's tone of authority, or that he should make the plans. But all the same what he had said was common sense. Noah would not want to be caught by the winter and the only way down the mountain was by the elephant track through the forest. They might come down it at any time.

The three collected their belongings, which they had hidden, filled the waterskin from the stream – unnecessary as it turned out in a mountainous country – and started walking. Soon they had to climb the hill beyond the lake. At last they reached the ridge and sat down to rest and look back. Two white spots – sheep, and brown ones – cattle, were picking their way over the stones by the lake shore. Then they could see the smoke of a fire and the tiny figures of men and women dotted about.

'You stay here tonight. I am going back,' said Gomer. They stared at him but would not demean themselves to ask a question, so after a little he had to tell them.

'I'm going back for the two Arab ponies,' said Gomer. 'I think they'll come with me, and once we have them nobody will be able to catch us.'

'Look out for yourself,' said Niss.

'Hadn't I better come too?' suggested Fan.

'No. One will be better than two. Don't worry. I shall creep near in the dark and wait till they are asleep. I don't think the dogs will bark if they scent me. They might if they heard me a long way off. With luck I shall be back before morning. If I am not, you had better go on alone, always keeping west.'

Once again Fan felt angry at the tone of authority in Gomer's voice. But what could she say? It would be giving Gomer more importance to say that without him there would be no future. Probably there was no future anyway. And it would be better to live and die by themselves than to become the slaves and mistresses of Ham and Shem. All the same she resented being told what to do by Gomer. He was gone while she still brooded over the authority in his voice: and he was a boy a year younger than she was.

The sisters built a fire out of sight of the Noahs, over the ridge and Niss made a soup of the mutton bone while Fan lay on the other side of the ridge to learn what she could of Noah's camp. Before it was dark she saw Japheth driving the sheep and cattle down to the camp by the lake and then Shem and Ham were helping to do something with them. Then it grew quite dark and there was nothing to be seen but the glowing spot of their fire. 'Two fires are burning on the whole earth,' she said to herself. 'And will there be none, or a dozen in thirty years' time?'

Next morning before it was really light they woke

to imagine that they had heard shouting down by the lake.

Then as the sun rose over the shoulder of Ararat, they heard a clattering of hoofs among the stones and the little grey stallion rushed up to the ridge and over it, shying when he saw them and the fire beyond and turning to whinny at the mare which followed with Gomer on her, riding bareback, but with his bare feet thrust into the ends of a length of narrow cloth which he had knotted and thrown doubled over her back. They packed up at once and went on, Fan and Niss taking turns in riding the mare, Gomer riding the stallion which was excitable and too difficult for them to manage. As they went down the wavering foothills into a wide valley they kept looking back but there was no sign of pursuit.

They camped beside a stream, and the girls hobbled the mare, made a fire and cooked the trout which Gomer had caught within a few minutes. With it they had a luxury they did not taste again for several years: a loaf of bread that Gomer had stolen out of the cooking tent while Noah was preaching a sermon. Gomer had listened to most of it and as they sat round the fire, he told Fan and Niss what he had heard.

Noah had talked to God and God had made a covenant with him in which He promised him that there should never be another Deluge. And as a sign He had set up the rainbow to remind Himself not to break His word.

He had told Noah that His orders to all the animals and to men and women were: 'Be fruitful and multiply.'

Gomer kept his eyes on the fire and did not look at either of the sisters as he spoke.

'I don't want to start multiplying. What do you feel Niss?' said Fan brutally.

'Not for a long time yet,' said Niss.

The Noahs would have to travel south-west to get back to Syria and Palestine, so Gomer and Fan decided to travel due west, following the bed of an immense upland valley along which ran the Euphrates river. The subsiding flood had choked the river banks with a barrage of trees and boulders, but the sides of the valley which had been pasture before the Deluge, were but little obstructed and the young grass was shooting everywhere, even though it was already autumn.

Fan would rise before dawn and set out in the first light carrying the fire drill and tinder and her own pack. Gomer and Niss would spend an hour or two longer asleep. When the sun was warm they would get up, unhobble the horses, load them with the tent and pots and pans, mount themselves and follow Fan. When they had ridden for two or three hours they would see a smoke somewhere ahead of them. That would be Fan. When they came up with her they would eat, the horses would be hobbled and turned out to graze and they would sleep. In the afternoon, Gomer would go down to the river and travel along until he could find a way through the broken trees to a place where he could fish. Meanwhile the sisters would pitch the tent and boil up a kettle of mushroom broth.

Every two or three days they had to stop and give Gomer time to fish and for the girls to collect wood mushrooms. They threaded them on a twig and dried them over the fire as a standby for the winter when they expected to be very short of food. There were no birds in the sky; no animals in the woods; no bushes grown enough to bear berries.

When Gomer was lucky in fishing they would gut and split the fish and dry them over the smoky fire. It would take a week to make a good job of drying them: but next morning they would pack the half-cured fish in one of Niss's woven rush baskets and move on and give it another cure that evening. They were uneasy until after they had reached the break in the mountains where the river turns on itself and runs southeast, on its way to Syria and Mesopotamia. For Gomer had heard his father say that Noah would follow the Euphrates. Once they had left the river behind, the going became more difficult. But there was no longer any hurry because of pursuit, but they were climbing slowly and they must be sure of getting out of the uplands before winter.

Actually they were caught in the first snowfall and were astonished to find themselves in a bare white world. It was not weather when anyone could hope to fish and the wood mushrooms were hidden under the snow and no more would appear until the following summer. Gomer rode ahead on the grey stallion; Niss followed leading the mare loaded with all their chattels, which increased every week. The sisters stripped the largest birches of their outer bark, cut it in strips and plaited baskets and saddle bags; saddles for the ponies; shoes and hats for themselves. Every few days they made themselves new possessions. Last of all came Fan, strolling along without a care in the world, following the footsteps in front of her and sometimes playing the reed pipe she had made.

It was cold, but the air was fresh and invigorating. How would they live if the ice covered the lakes so that they could not fish? Their half-cured fish and dried mushrooms would not last them for more than a few weeks.

In that white world they felt their loneliness upon the earth. It was a comfort when the ponies sought company and often came nuzzling the backs of their necks when they sat by the fire.

Gomer rode every day, just to keep the stallion exercised, and sometimes Niss would go and look out from a high point over the white world and then, if the mare ran up to her as she walked back to the camp, she would put her arms round the brown neck and bury her cold cheek in the rough mane.

The snow melted and fell again trapping them in their tent while the blizzard lasted. Then they went

on, doubtful and hungry in the silent world. And then
suddenly, after they came over a rise, they saw the sea
before them – and far away – across it, the outline of
snow-covered hills. There was a beach, free of snow,
all pebbles and with entanglements of driftwood where
rocks ran into the sea. Leaving Gomer and Niss to
pitch the tent and unload, Fan forced her way through
the driftwood to find that there were rockpools beyond,
in which little crabs scurried to shelter and grey
prawns retreated backwards and disappeared. Their
food supply was solved.

All that winter they lived by the sea shore, travelling
slowly south in search of warmth, stopping for a few
days if they found the fishing was good. For the first
time since leaving the ark they saw animals and birds:
ducks and seagulls of different sizes, otters, seals and
sometimes a school of dolphins. But away from the
water they did not see any four-footed beast, not a
lizard, not a tortoise, not a snake. But the sea was
crammed with fish. By the spring they were in a
warmer climate: the grass came up lush and thick
with wild cyclamens among the rocks and wild narcissi
and daffodils in the damp pastures. As it grew warmer
they discarded their sheepskin cloaks and went nearly
naked. Every day the girls went swimming and at last,
thanks to their jeering, Gomer had the courage to
imitate them.

Niss held him under the chin and swam with him,
teaching him the breast stroke. Fan lay on her back

floating and cried out: 'Like this! Like this,' as she used the back stroke with her arms and gave a scissors kick with her legs. Then she would make Gomer lie on his back and swim with him with her hands on each side of his ears.

The sun shone: the brackish sea water tasted queer and splashed into Gomer's eyes: there was a tangle of the girls' wet hair, the flashing of their eager grey eyes and the mewing of a seagull overhead. Gomer lay in the sun on the sand between them exhausted, but he soon learned. They were happy.

One hot night in the early summer their mare had a foal, a filly, marbled grey in colour.

Two years later when that foal was herself with foal the two girls were sitting by the fire, Niss weaving a lobster pot out of osier and Fan chipping flint to make an eel-spear. The two sisters had changed without knowing it. Both had grown into beautiful young women, tall and high-breasted; their hair was long and silky and they often washed it in fresh water with the ash from burned seaweed which took out the grease, after which, every hair separate, it fell about their clear oval faces from which the grey eyes looked out mischievously.

But while at the beginning of this story Fan and Niss had been so much alike that they were constantly being mistaken for one another, after they left the ark they grew apart.

Fan was taller than Niss, her cheeks redder, her hair

a darker shade of brown. Niss's hair had touches of gold in it. Her skin was paler, her voice softer, her smile gentler and when she smiled she showed her teeth more than Fan.

Gomer had altered also. His voice was deeper. But though he had acquired the assurance of a man, he was gentler and he and Fan never disputed about leadership because he cared nothing about being leader – only about doing their daily work in the best way. Niss often let her eyes linger on his naked body, but he seemed unaware of it, and nothing in his manner revealed that he loved one sister more than the other – and yet though it was unspoken, each of the three knew that he loved Niss in a different way from Fan.

While Niss bent and twisted the willow rods she was thinking about Gomer, and that she could not tell Fan what she felt about him, ever.

'Blast it,' said Fan throwing away the flint which had broken across the point. Then she lifted her eyes and saw a dark man walking towards them from the south along the seashore.

'Look Niss,' she whispered and Niss looked up and saw him. He was limping. He was the first man except Gomer they had seen since they had taken that last look at Noah's family beside the lake, while Gomer was crawling down on them to steal the stallion and the mare.

The young man looked up and saw them sitting there and came towards them. He was Ham's son

Mizraim. They looked at him but said nothing. Mizraim threw himself down on the grass beside them and he said only:

'So I have found you.'

'Where are the others?' asked Niss.

'I don't know. I ran away from them and came to find you.'

Fan saw that he was spent with travel so she put aside the stone she was knapping and brought him a cup of mare's milk and Mizraim drank it without thanking her and put his head down on the turf and slept.

He was still sleeping when Gomer came back with five fish he had caught.

He looked at Mizraim queerly and at once asked the same question as Niss. 'Where are the others?'

'Mizraim ran away from them and has come a long way looking for us.'

'He may be lying and be Noah's spy,' said Gomer.

'He is telling the truth,' said Fan watching Gomer's face.

'If I killed him now we could be certain that he would never go back and tell where we are.'

Niss gutted the five fish and laid them on the flat stone in the middle of the embers.

'Two men are better than one,' said Fan.

Mizraim woke up and stretched and rubbed his eyes.

'Come and eat,' said Niss, bringing the fish up from the fire. They ate slowly picking the bones out with their fingers. Occasionally Gomer looked at Mizraim as though by accident and Mizraim looked back, expressionless through lowered eyelids.

'What was it that made you come in search of us?' asked Niss.

'It was old Noah. When we got to the edge of the mountain and the plain and the sea, Noah told us that we should settle there. It was a good place indeed, with the sea for fishing, pasture for our flocks and stone and timber for building. Noah had brought seed corn and slips of vines and he planted a vineyard along the lowest slope of the hill while my father and my uncles ploughed a level field below and sowed wheat and barley and millet and the women made their gardens.

'Everything flourished. There were no birds or beetles or rabbits to peck and pierce and gnaw the crops. The first autumn we had enough corn to make bread and porridge. Last autumn Noah had his first grapes. That made him mad. He watched them all the summer, then when he picked them, I had to tread the bunches all day long in a tub.

'It was about six months after the wine was made that one sabbath he did not show up for evening prayers. My father went first to the cave where he kept the jars of wine, then, as he wasn't there, he went to the vineyard, where the vines were just coming into leaf. There was Grandpapa, dead drunk, lying naked in the last rays of the setting sun.

'Father thought it was a joke to be laughed off: he

went and called my uncles. Father thought it funny they should all be assembled waiting for the evening prayer while the old man was lying there naked and sozzled. But my uncles were terribly shocked. Japheth cried out that it was an accident and they took a cloak and covered up their father without looking at him. But my father went on making a joke of it and asking them how they could cover him without looking to see where he was. I suppose Shem must have told the old man about it, because next morning while I was lying enjoying the sabbath rest with my father and brothers, Grandpapa came up in a flaming rage and started to curse us. He cursed my brother Canaan and my father and all the rest of us and said we were to be slaves for evermore and do all the rough work for Japheth and Shem and for all their descendants. We should be bought and sold as slaves. And it was to be for ever and ever. Do you know he talked then just as though he were God?

'My Dad said that Grandpapa would get over it and take the curse off us. But he didn't. Next day Shem started ordering us about and when Canaan told him to shut up and clear out, Shem and his sons came and tied up my brother and whipped him until the blood was running down his back.

'I wasn't going to stand for that. I had been thinking about you ever since you went and wishing I had had the courage to go with you. Then I kept wondering how I could find you. There was all the earth for me to look for you in. And then that night after they flogged Canaan, lying awake I got an idea. I thought that you would have been sure to do what we had done, that is, walk until you got to the sea, where you could get a living fishing. Because you had no goats and cows to milk and no sheep. So you must be living on fish. I knew you were north of us and I thought if I followed the coast I must find you. And that's why I am here.'

It was dark. The fire was only a glow of embers. Gomer yawned.

The two girls got up and wandered off: they slept close together that night and were silent. The boys lay by the fire but they were distrustful of each other and for some time lay awake listening and hearing nothing but the sudden unexpected wave breaking on the beach and dragging back the shingle.

Next morning the girls had blown up the fire before the boys awoke and when they did wake they were alone and Fan and Niss were visible far out in the shallows by the rocks shrimping.

Later on Mizraim walked down to where Gomer was mending his fishing line and squatted beside him.

'What's the fishing like?' he asked.

'So so.'

'As I came up the coast I could see a lot of islands out at sea.'

'What of it?'

'If we went off to an island nobody could come near us.'

[141]

'How would you get there?' asked Gomer.

'We might build a boat. It would be good for fishing too.'

'By golly,' said Gomer.

'If that lot could build the ark we could build us a little boat that would sail on the sea. And we wouldn't take twenty years about it either,' said Mizraim.

'Let's get on with it,' said Gomer.

The temper of the two lads changed and when the girls came back and called to them, they were half a mile along the shore dragging out driftwood.

After that they kept away from the girls while they were working, only coming back to the camp for meals. When Niss said that they needed more fish, Gomer grumbled and told her to go and catch it herself. However, afterwards he set some nightlines along the shore and Mizraim went and helped Fan carry in some firewood from the broken forest. But they did not volunteer anything about their work and the girls were too proud to ask questions.

Mizraim's coming had changed the happy unquestioning relationship between Gomer and the sisters. One day when the boys were working together hauling out seasoned tree trunks, Mizraim looked up and said:

'Niss is your girl, isn't she?'

Gomer looked at him and nodded.

'Well, I'll take Fan.'

'That's up to her, mate,' said Gomer, grinning suddenly. Actually the idea that Niss was his girl and that

Fan wasn't was a new one – and somehow it missed the point of their relationship and spoilt it. But with Mizraim there it could not be helped and anyhow there was the boat to build and seas and islands to explore, which would not have been possible without him.

The first craft they put together was a raft with tree trunks lashed together with withies of willow. They poled it about along the shore. The girls swam out and climbed on and when Fan dived from it, Mizraim lost his balance and fell in and was laughed at because he nearly got drowned and was angry. Later on Fan taught him to swim and soon he was better than any of them in the water. This was a consolation to him for he was lame on land and could not run like the others. The raft was heavy and though it made a good platform for fishing, it was no good as a boat.

The next craft was a catamaran made with two tree trunks kept apart by crosspieces. Gomer sat on one side, Mizraim on the other and they paddled along. But a sail was wanted and eventually the girls made one of interwoven flags. This matting sail was heavy and clumsy but it caught the wind and in a stiff breeze they could go fast and rest from paddling. After they had tried it out they shifted camp, Mizraim and Fan sailing and paddling down the coast, Gomer and Niss riding the stallion and the mare with the two-year-old and the young foal trotting beside them.

The horsemen and fishermen who first went down

into Greece were their great-grandchildren and great-great-grandchildren. They worshipped the Python at Delphi and made a god of the poet Apollo. They carried on the tradition which Noah had thought so shocking, that the angels, or the gods, fell in love with princesses and shepherd girls and were the fathers of the most beautiful and most exceptional of the human race. They were not jealous of such strange matings but gloried in them. But long before that time the lizards had come back upon the rocks, the bees were storing honey from thyme and cistus and the young people had traded horses for goats and sheep and cattle and pearls for vines with Noah's kingdom and they had hounds for hunting and to guard their flocks against the wolves. But that is no longer the story of Fan and Niss, but the history of mankind.

6

3.4.74